TRUTH SEEKER

Deborah Lisson

PB

THE O'BRIEN PRESS
DUBLIN

First published 2001 by The O'Brien Press Ltd.,
20 Victoria Road, Rathgar, Dublin 6, Ireland.
Tel: +353 1 4923333; Fax: +353 1 4922777
E-mail: books@obrien.ie
Website: www.obrien.ie

ISBN: 0-86278-701-7

British Library Cataloguing-in-Publication Data
Lisson, Deborah
Truth seeker
1.Vikings - Ireland - Juvenile fiction 2.Adventure stories
3.Children's stories
I.Title
823[J]

1 2 3 4 5 6 7 8 9 10
01 02 03 04 05 06 07 08 09 10

The O'Brien Press receives
assistance from

Editing, typesetting, layout, design: The O'Brien Press Ltd.
Cover separations: C&A Print Services Ltd.
Printing: Guernsey Press Ltd.

TRUTHSEEKER

DEBORAH LISSON was born in England and grew up in East Anglia, in a little village about half way between Ipswich and Norwich. She emigrated to Australia in 1963 and after spending some time in Sydney, moved to Western Australia where she still lives. Deborah has five grown-up children and eleven grandchildren. She and her husband now live in Bunbury, a coastal town about a hundred miles from Perth. Deborah is a well-known writer in Australia. *Red Hugh*, the story of Red Hugh O'Donnell's escape from Dublin Castle, was the first of her books to be published in Ireland. It won a Western Australian Premier's Prize.

DEDICATION

Remembering Eye National School and 'Billy' Bourne
for whom I wrote my first stories.

ICELAND

NORWAY

Agdir

SWEDEN

SCOTLAND

North Sea

Sigfrid's home

Aggersborg

IRELAND

Lindisfarne

DENMARK

Dublin
(Dubh Linn)

York

Hedeby

ENGLAND

WALES

Thetford   Hellesdon
          Hoxne

FRISIA

Beodricesworth
(Bury St Edmunds)

London

FRANCE

CONTENTS

Author's Note

Writing a novel based on the lives of real people during the Viking age is a tricky business. There are no newspaper cuttings from the period, no old television footage or radio broadcasts. A novelist has to rely on the historians. But historians are concerned with trying to provide the truest possible account of what *really* happened. They present different theories and draw different conclusions. It can all get very complicated. My task is to sift through all the theories, find the interesting characters and the events that would have made the newspapers, and make an engaging story out of the possibilities. It's a bit like being a detective!

And, luckily, a novelist has a little more leeway than the historian. She is not required to say, 'This is the truth, the whole truth and nothing but the truth,' only, 'This is the truth, the possible truth and the nobody-can-absolutely-prove-it-isn't truth.' As long as my readers understand the difference, no one can complain.

1

ESCAPE FROM DENMARK

From a corner of the hall, as far as he could remove himself from the high seat, Sigfrid watched the entertainment at his stepfather's spring feast. Arne Brodirsson had possession of the harp and was singing one of the ancient sagas. It was a sad song. Sigfrid knew it by heart, but still he listened with rapt attention. It told how Balder, son of Odin and the most beloved of all the gods, was killed through the trickery of Loki Mischief-Maker and carried off to the underworld realm of Niflheim by the giantess Hel.

Arne's voice was rich and strong and carried

effortlessly into every corner of the hall while his hands, tough and callused from his years at sea, touched the harpstrings with a surprising lightness. *'When all things weep for Odin's son, then Hel will yield up her hostage,'* sang Arne, and Sigfrid held his breath as if, somehow, by his willing it, the story could be made to end differently this time. But of course it couldn't. For a while things looked promising as, one by one, every creature, living and dead, shed tears for the beautiful Balder, but inexorably the narrative led at last to one grim and gloomy cave and a giantess who spoke the fatal words: *'Alive or dead, what use to me, the War God's whelp? Let Hel hold what she has.'* The harp quivered for a moment, a cascade of notes spilling like tears over the assembly, and faded into silence.

There was a moment's stillness. Then the audience sighed as one man and shook itself back to reality. A loud cheer went through the hall and a horn of mead was brought to cool the singer's throat. Arne held out the harp, inviting someone else to take it, but his audience was unwilling to let him go.

'Give us another tale,' they begged. 'Sing us "The Otter's Ransom".'

'Tell of your own adventures,' shouted someone. 'Of how you went a-viking to Ireland last summer. About Dublin, and the exploits of Ivar Ragnarsson. Tell us …'

He stopped. There was a deathly silence and all eyes

turned towards the high seat. Hoskuld came to his feet with a roar. 'Who dares to speak in my hall of Ivar Ragnarsson?' he bellowed. 'What good has that Odin-worshipping berserker ever done for any of you? He sits over there in Dublin and calls himself a king, but who tends the farm he deserted in his greed for fame? Who married his wife? Who feeds and clothes the brat he left behind when he abandoned her? It is I, Hoskuld, who puts food in your mouths and clothes on your backs. And it is my Gods – Freyr and the Vanir – who protect this farm. And let none of you forget it.'

Sigfrid listened to the tirade in white-faced fury. What a bag of wind, he thought. What a coward. He had an overwhelming urge to snatch up his drinking horn and throw it and its contents into his stepfather's blustering face. But he restrained himself – he knew from painful experience what the result of such defiance would be.

Yes, he would take on a boy, but he hasn't the guts to do what my real father did, Sigfrid thought. Ivar won his kingdom at the point of his sword while Hoskuld … hah, he has never fought a battle in his life. He came creeping down here out of Sweden ten years ago and wriggled like a snake into my mother's affections. Now, in his shame, he cannot bear to hear my father's name.

Sigfrid's hand crept up to touch the amulet he wore around his neck. It was a silver pendant, shaped like the hammer of Thor, and inscribed with the runes for strength and protection. His mother had given it to him and told him it had belonged to his father. It was the only thing of Ivar's he possessed and he would have died before parting with it.

Hoskuld, his good humour restored by his outburst, sat down again. Thralls had appeared from the kitchen bearing platters of meat – horseflesh from the sacred stallion that had been ritually slaughtered that afternoon. As they carried the platters from table to table, Sigfrid felt his lip curl in disgust. Horsemeat! The traditional spring sacrifice to Freyr, the fertility God. Why should we sacrifice to Freyr? he wondered indignantly. We are not Swedes. We are Danes, warriors. Thor is our God, and Odin the Allfather. What do we want with Hoskuld's Gods?

He glanced round the hall, to see if anyone else agreed with him, but the company was too busy eating. He looked at his mother. How can she live with him? he wondered. How can she not despise him, when she compares him to my father? But Gudrun, smiling, plump and cossetted at Hoskuld's side, seemed unaware of her husband's shortcomings. Sigfrid sighed. Then his eye caught Arne's. The Viking winked at him and there was something so conspiratorial in the gesture that the boy felt his spirits rise. He was not quite alone, after all. Someone did understand. And Arne knew his father; he had met him, talked with him in Ireland. Arne would be able to tell him all the things he needed to know.

He determined to speak to the Viking, but before the chance presented itself, Arne rose and asked to take his leave. 'I thank you for your hospitality, Hoskuld Torfinsson,' he said, 'but I must return to my ship at Aggersborg. The winds and the tides are favourable and my crew is waiting for me. We sail in the morning.'

He didn't say where they were going but everyone in the hall knew.

Sigfrid sat through the rest of the evening in silence, staring into the fire that burned in a long grate down the centre of the hall. In the white-hot caverns amid the burning logs, he fancied he saw images of Ireland – mountains and valleys, shining, blue-green rivers, the great lough where Ivar had fought and won a three day battle against Norwegian rivals soon after his arrival. He saw monasteries where black-clad followers of the White Christ sat over their treasure like old and toothless dragons but fled in terror before the swords of brave Viking heroes. He saw the mighty hall overlooking the black pool, *Dubh Linn*, where Ivar now sat in state with his fellow king, the Norwegian, Olaf Guthrothsson.

'I am the son of the king of Dublin,' he told himself silently, and cursed the cruel twist of fate that meant that one of his standing should have to work the land like a thrall – a slave – for a man whose sword had never tasted blood and whose idea of greatness was to slaughter a horse for Freyr.

The feast ended early. Tomorrow the games would start. There would be horse races, archery and spear-throwing contests, and savage and often lethal stallion fights. Everyone wanted to be up bright-eyed and eager for the fun. Hoskuld and Gudrun retired to their private bed cubicle. Visitors – those who could still walk – were shown to the guest hall, and the rest of the company bedded down on mattresses laid out by thralls on the wide, fixed benches that ran down each side of the great hall.

Sigfrid found sleep impossible. He lay on his bench, listening to the snoring and snuffling all around him and thought about Arne Brodirsson, riding back to his ship. There were boats here at the farm, small, sturdy little fishing vessels, but nothing to compare with a craft like Arne's. *Seasnake*, he had said her name was, and Sigfrid could picture her, sleek and sinuous as a serpent, her prow upswept like a new-drawn sword, her fierce, carved dragon head shining in the sun as she took the wind in her sail and flew across the sea. West-over-seas she would go, west with the Viking wind, onward and onward, until ...

Suddenly Sigfrid could bear it no more. He sat up, wild

ideas chasing through his head. Why shouldn't he? Nobody would miss him before morning – listen to how they were all snoring! And if they did, why would anyone care? His mother might weep for him, but Hoskuld would probably be glad to see the back of him.

A little voice in his head reminded him that this was not strictly true. Hoskuld had reared him all through his useless, childhood years. Now that he was fourteen and could do a man's work about the farm, his stepfather doubtless expected a return on that investment.

No, when he was discovered missing there would be a furious hue and cry, and if Hoskuld caught him … well, it didn't bear thinking about, so Sigfrid refused to think of it. His mind was made up. He would take one of the swiftest horses in the stables and by the time daylight came he could be in Aggersborg with Arne Brodirsson. Of course, Arne might refuse to take him, but Sigfrid didn't think he would. The man was a Viking. He had winked at Sigfrid, understood the longing in his heart. Arne Brodirsson would take him to his father.

With infinite care Sigfrid picked his way across the floor, stepping over the sprawled bodies of sleepers who had been unable – or too drunk – to find a space on the benches. At the back of the hall, he hesitated outside the partitioned-off corner that was the private bed-closet of Hoskuld and Gudrun. A daring thought was forming in his mind. Apart from the horse he planned to steal, he would be leaving the farm with nothing, not even a spare shirt. He was content that this should be so, but there was one thing without which a would-be Viking could not survive: his sword.

Sigfrid did not possess a sword, but Hoskuld did. The beautiful, double-edged Rhenish blade with a silver hilt had lain on the table before him, in a place of honour, all through the feast, the weapon with which he had slain the sacrificial stallion. The honour of Hoskuld's family resided in that sword. His great grandfather had won land and riches with it and his grandfather had died with it in his hand, defending his king against invaders. Hoskuld boasted constantly of the blood it had drunk and the victories it had gained. He treated it like a precious icon. One of Sigfrid's duties had been to clean and polish it until it gleamed and to oil the leather scabbard in which it hung. Sigfrid loved that sword. He grieved for its lost glory, for it had won little fame in Hoskuld's keeping. What courage did it take to kill a horse? Was animal blood an honourable substitute for the wound-gold of an enemy?

A man like Hoskuld did not deserve so beautiful a weapon. He, Sigfrid, would liberate it, would give it back its dignity and use it in the manner for which it had been created. In his hands it would win fame and glory and riches beyond imagining. Why, it was more than his right to take it, it was his sacred duty.

Convinced by his own eloquence, he eased open the door of the bed-closet and crept in. He knew exactly where the sword would be. Every night Hoskuld drew it from its scabbard and hung it, naked, in ritual guardianship above his bed. To reach it, Sigfrid would have to stand on tiptoe and lean right over his snoring stepfather. At the bedside he hesitated. He looked down into the sleeping face. He looked up at the sword; he thought of *Seasnake* waiting for him at Aggersborg. Was it worth the risk? If his stepfather woke, the great adventure would be over before it had even started and Hoskuld would half-kill him for his audacity.

But he wanted that blade. He lusted after it. He could feel the weight of it in his hand, the fit of the scabbard around his hips. And he had to have a weapon. Without it he was nothing. Who would take seriously an unarmed fourteen-year-old? Swiftly, before his courage could desert him, he reached up to claim his weapon.

The sword seemed almost to leap into his hand and nestled there, cool and deadly like a viper. He picked up the scabbard from the chest at the foot of the bed and was about to slide the blade into it when, suddenly, Gudrun stirred. She mumbled, rolled onto her back and her eyes flickered opened. They stared at Sigfrid, then moved to the sword which he held in his hand – comprehension slowly dawning.

Sigfrid froze. For a long moment mother and son looked at each other; her gaze seemed to search every corner of Sigfrid's heart. She was reading him as a seer reads the runes. He wanted to plead with her, to beg for understanding, but his tongue seemed frozen in his mouth. For an agony of time he watched her helplessly. Then his mother smiled, the softest, tiniest flicker of a smile, closed her eyes, and turned onto her side again.

Sigfrid rammed the blade into its scabbard and fled for the stables. He knew the horse he wanted and where its gear was kept. Within minutes he was mounted and riding for his life down the track to Aggersborg. At the top of the first hill he turned for one last, fearful glance behind him, but everything was still. The farm slept, a huddle of shadowy buildings under the glitter of the stars.

2

A VIKING IN DUBLIN

'So,' said Ivar Ragnarsson, eyeing his new-found son much as one might a stray puppy presented for inspection. 'So, this is what I begat all those years ago, is it?'

Sigfrid's heart lurched. He felt clumsy and tongue-tied. This wasn't how it was supposed to be. All the way from Denmark he had fantasised about this meeting. Had his imagination cheated him? This man is my father, he reminded himself, the man who gave life to me. Surely he must feel something for me? He searched the older man's features, seeking some resemblance – some image of himself that he might recognise – but there was nothing. It was like looking into a mask hacked out of granite.

'And they call you Sigfrid, eh?'

He nodded.

'And how old would you be now? Fifteen?'

Another nod – a silent lie.

'So, almost a man. And I suppose your stepfather has sent you out into the world to make your fortune?'

'Him? Hah! He would keep me on the farm, working like a thrall. I ran away.'

'Did you now?' For the first time a tiny smile chipped the corners of the mask. 'And, tell me, what directed your feet west-over-seas to Ireland?'

He is mocking me, thought the boy, and despite everything he felt his temper rising. Nobody poked fun at Sigfrid Ivarsson. 'In Denmark, the skalds make extravagant songs about the deeds of Ivar Ragnarsson,' he said haughtily. 'I came to see if they were true.'

There was a silence. For a moment he feared he had gone too far. Then Ivar roared with laughter. 'Your songmakers speak the truth,' he said. 'The ravens who feast where I have passed can tell you that.' He took a step forward, the granite mask dissolved into flesh and blood, and suddenly Sigfrid found himself embraced in a huge bear-hug. 'You are welcome in my hall, Sigfrid

TruthSeeker. You are not afraid to speak your mind, and that is good. I do not beget sons to become milksops!'

Ivar went to the door and bellowed for a thrall to bring ale, then waved Sigfrid to a bench. 'Sit down,' he said, 'and tell me of your adventures. I know that Arne Brodirsson brought you here. He is a good man. Where did you meet him? How fares your mother? Does the farm prosper?'

Sigfrid tried to answer the questions but they skipped across his brain like pebbles across water. A drum of triumph was beating in his head. You have done it, it boomed. You have escaped. No more drudgery, no more dishonour. You have journeyed west-over-seas to the hall of the King of Dublin, and he has acknowledged you as his son.

Dazed with happiness, he looked at the banner on the wall above the high seat. It depicted a raven, black and deadly, with wings outstretched in flight. It had a history, that banner. The songmakers said it had belonged to Ivar's father, the legendary Ragnar Lodbrok, and that its stirrings could foretell victory for its owner. It was at rest now, there was no breeze in the hall to give it life. But one day, thought Sigfrid, one day … and the hairs on the back of his neck prickled at the prospect. Without his realising it, his hand slid out to touch the sword he had unbuckled and laid on the table when he first came in.

His father noticed the movement and smiled. 'Your own?' he asked.

'Yes.' Sigfrid did not see the need to elaborate.

'So.' Ivar drew the weapon from its scabbard and held it up to the flickering torchlight, squinting along its length. 'A fine blade,' he pronounced. 'Have you blooded it yet?'

Sigfrid shook his head.

'You will,' said Ivar. He looked sternly at his son. 'Sword and axe, let you remember them; they are the weapons of a Viking. But to a king's son, it is his sword brings greatest honour. The axe is the hammer of Thor. It lusts for plunder. It hacks and slashes like a scythe through barley, and never counts its kills. But the sword is Odin's. When you give a man to Odin at the point of your sword – when you look into his eyes and see that he reads his death reflected in your own – then you will understand the meaning of victory.'

Sigfrid nodded. He thought of Hoskuld, who had never killed a man in his life, and of the honour he would now bring to his stepfather's cheated sword. What does it feel like, he wanted to ask, to give a man to Odin? How many men have seen their death written in your eyes? But before he could find the right words the door opened and a man entered the room. He was tall and fair – a rangy, rawboned man with blue eyes and a mane of white-gold hair. He approached the table with an air of arrogant confidence and Sigfrid guessed at once who he must be: Olaf Guthrothsson, sometimes called Olaf the White, leader of the Norwegian faction in Dublin and Ivar's fellow king.

Ivar introduced them.

'So,' said the Norwegian. 'Your son, eh? You are a lucky man, Ivar Ragnarsson.' He ruffled Sigfrid's hair and grinned at him. 'And what adventure has brought you west-over-seas, young Sigfrid – some unspeakable deed in Denmark that has left you outlawed?'

'Certainly not!' The teasing remark was too close to the bone for comfort. Could you be outlawed for stealing the icon of a man's honour? 'I came as any man comes who follows the gulls' path – to seek fame and fortune. I am a king's son. I grew tired of life on a farm.'

'Ah,' said Olaf. 'A king's son.' He smiled again, but this time the smile didn't quite reach his eyes. 'I, too have a son,' he said softly, 'by a daughter of the Irish High King. Did they tell you that?'

Sigfrid swallowed. There was a silence in the room that you could have stuck a dagger into. It occurred to him that his whole future in Ireland possibly depended on what he said next. He took a deep breath. 'Then you, too, are a lucky man, Olaf Guthrothsson, for no doubt your son will make a fine king in Dublin, when the time

23

comes. As for me … I mean to make my fortune here at the sword's edge, and return in triumph to Denmark.'

Olaf looked at him intently. Then a broad grin spread across his face and Sigfrid knew he had passed the test. He grinned too, but doubt stuck in his heart. Could he ever go back to Denmark? Might Hoskuld in his rage have had him declared 'wolfshead' – an outlaw whom any man might kill?

The Norwegian sat down 'A shrewd head on such youthful shoulders,' he chuckled approvingly, and poured himself a beaker of ale. 'Your health, Sigfrid Ivarsson, you are welcome in Dublin. But now, you must leave us. I have urgent matters to discuss with your father.'

Sigfrid rose. 'Go and find Arne,' instructed his father. 'Tell him he is to find you food and then show you around the settlement. I shall be busy for the rest of the day, but tonight we shall feast your coming in the hall.'

In the novelty of exploring his new home, Sigfrid soon forgot his anxieties about what might be happening in his old one. The Viking encampment at Dublin was built on a peninsula formed by two rivers that flowed out into a large, sheltered bay. It had started, Arne explained, as a small encampment on the shores of the *Dubh Linn*, the black pool, that had gradually spread northward and westward as more and more adventurers had decided to make it their permanent base rather than sail back to Scandinavia each winter. Ivar's hall was the original one, built years before by a long-dead warrior named Thorgils. It overlooked the black pool, where the Danish ships were beached. Olaf had established his hall and his own *longphort* on the other river, the Liffey. According to Arne, it was an arrangement that worked well. Each king was a regular visitor in the hall of the other, but by keeping their ships and followers apart, they managed to avoid tensions and rivalries that might otherwise have threatened their alliance.

To Sigfrid, fresh from life on a farm, Dublin was a confusing cacophony of sights and sounds and smells. The warm spring weather had brought a horde of new arrivals and he thought he had never seen so many people crammed together in one spot. He wondered if he would ever find his way around with the easy confidence of Arne and stuck close to his side as the Viking led him through the higgledy-piggledy maze of laneways. He was half afraid that if he lost sight of him he might never find his way out again.

There were buildings of every type and size; some old and weathered, some new, some still under construction. Many of the larger houses reminded Sigfrid of the farmhouse he had left behind in Denmark. They were stave-built, their walls constructed from long planks pressed tightly together and set in an upright position. Others were similar, but with planks set horizontally, while many more, particularly the smaller ones, were timber-framed with panels of wattle and daub. They looked as if they had been woven on some giant's loom and then plastered over with mud to keep the draught out. The strangest ones – and there were only a handful of these – were round, with a thatched roof that rose to a steep point in the middle. Arne said they were of an Irish design.

Scattered among the houses were workshops and the small huts, called *bothies*, that were used by tradesmen. They passed a cooper's shop and a carpenter's and a bakehouse where the baker was drawing loaves from a big stone oven. The bread was baked on flat, long-handled pans. The baker pulled them from the oven one by one, tipped the loaves out onto a table, slapped fresh chunks of dough on the pans and slid them back into the oven again. The new loaves were brown and crusty and the smell rising from them was tantalizing. Sigfrid felt his stomach growl. Arne grinned at him.

'Hungry?'

He nodded. Arne fished a small chunk of silver from his pouch and exchanged it for a couple of loaves. He gave one to Sigfrid. 'Don't eat it all at once,' he warned. 'I'm taking you to visit a friend of mine and we'll get a proper meal there.'

'Who is this friend?' asked Sigfrid, as they set off again through more winding, wood-paved alleyways, past more rows of tightly packed houses.

'Guthrum Brusasson. He is a wood carver, and he is making something for me – something very special. He has been working on it all winter while I've been away. Ah, here we are,' He stopped before a large building. 'Come in and I'll introduce you.'

He pushed open the door and Sigfrid found himself in a long room, with a bench running down one side. There was a window over the bench, its wooden shutter thrown wide open. Beneath it a man, Guthrum, he supposed, was bent over, working at something on the bench with a chisel and a small hammer. The floor at his feet was covered with woodshavings, and all around the room were the products of his craft: stools, benches, a bedstead, and two huge table tops, all embellished with intricate and extravagant designs. In one corner stood a pile of roughly-dressed timber and beside it, propped against the wall …

'Arne! Arne Brodirsson!' Guthrum had looked up and seen them and was pumping Arne's hand as if he would pull his arm off. 'It's good to see you again, old friend. Now I know the winter is truly over. Have you told Gráinne you are here?' Without waiting for a reply he stuck his head out of the window and shouted something in a strange sing-song language. A woman's voice answered him. 'She gives you a hundred thousand welcomes and will have food and drink prepared in no time,' he said. 'We must celebrate your arrival. And who is this with you? Surely not your son?'

'No,' laughed Arne. He introduced Sigfrid and Guthrum greeted him courteously.

'It is an honour to have the king's son in my home.'

Sigfrid shook his hand. 'Arne said you were making something for him. Is it ... ?' He gestured towards the corner.

'Indeed it is. Come, see what you think of it, if it is worth all the gold Arne promised me.' He led them both over to his new creation and Sigfrid felt a shiver of sheer wonder run down his spine. He was looking at the most magnificent dragon-head he had ever seen.

'A gift for *Seasnake*,' said Arne softly, and he too gazed in wonder at the figurehead. Sigfrid saw how perfectly Guthrum had matched his design to the name of the ship. The head he had created was fierce but not overlarge, and set on a long slender neck. The mouth, each fang-like tooth individually carved, gaped in a terrible, frozen snarl, the nostrils flared and the eyes glared from fiercely bulging sockets. Around the head and up and down the neck ran a serpentine pattern of 'gripping beasts', strange creatures with sinuous bodies, thickened fore and hind quarters, and claws that clutched both themselves and each other and the frames into which they were set.

Sigfrid had seen similar carvings before – the gripping beast was a popular motif – but he had never seen the design so exquisitely rendered. He tried to trace one of the lines with his finger, but so intricate was the inter-weaving that it was almost impossible to tell where one creature began and another ended. It seemed astonish-ing to Sigfrid that a piece of work so graceful and delicate when studied at close range could produce so fearsome an overall effect. Guthrum was truly a master craftsman.

Arne was delighted with his new purchase. He paid Guthrum with an arm-ring of plaited gold and said he would send some of his men to carry it down to his ship. Then they all went into Guthrum's house, next door to his workshop, to celebrate the transaction.

The woman, Gráinne, was waiting at the door to wel-come them. She was small and pretty with dark hair, smooth milk-white skin and the deepest blue eyes Sig-frid had ever seen. Arne whispered to Sigfrid that she was Irish. Guthrum had bought her as a slave two years ago but had since married her. She seemed an unlikely wife for the brawny, blonde Scandinavian, but they were clearly very happy together. At Guthrum's insistence she showed them the beautiful piece of woollen cloth, half finished on her loom, which she told them was going to make a cloak for Guthrum, a special gift to mark the second anniversary of their marriage.

She spoke in Irish and her husband translated for her. He explained that although she understood most of what was said to her, she still could not speak the Norse tongue with any fluency.

'But I learn,' Gráinne said carefully. Then, with a smile and a gesture, she indicated one of the benches running the full length of the wall. When they had seated themselves, she brought them bread and cheese and bowls of mutton broth which she ladled from the big cauldron hanging over the hearth in the centre of the room.

Sigfrid ate eagerly and listened while Arne and Guthrum caught up on all their news and exchanged gossip about mutual acquaintances. 'So,' said Guthrum, 'when we last met, you told me that it was in your mind to build a hall for yourself and your ship-companions and make your base here. Is that still your plan?'

Arne grinned. 'It is. My father died last winter, and my brother has the farm. There is nothing now to keep me in Denmark. I have decided to throw in my lot with Ivar.'

'Then we must drink to that.' Guthrum spoke to Gráinne and she fetched drinking horns into which she poured measures of a strange-smelling, tawny-coloured wine.

'To new adventures,' said Guthrum, 'and to *Seasnake* and her new dragon-head. May she carry you to fame and fortune.'

He tossed off his drink in one gulp, and Arne followed suit. Not to be outdone, Sigfrid copied them. It was like swallowing liquid fire. His mouth stung, fumes seared his nose and throat; he thought his head was going to explode. He coughed and spluttered and tears streamed down his face. Gráinne had to run and fetch him water.

'Loki's beard!' he gasped when he could speak again. 'What is this stuff?'

'Usquebaugh,' said Guthrum. He was laughing so hard he could hardly answer. 'It is an Irish drink. They make it from barley and its name means "the water of life".'

'Water of life? It tastes more like dragons' blood!'

'You'll get used to it. It is excellent for keeping out the winter cold. Here,' he poured another measure, 'try some more, only this time drink it more slowly.'

Sigfrid sipped tentatively and found that once you got used to its fiery bite the drink did indeed leave a very pleasant glow. My first taste of Dublin, he thought, and wondered what other surprises this new life held for him.

Ivar's hall had been transformed for the evening feast and

nothing at home could have prepared Sigfrid for such magnificence. Torches and candles infused the long room with a rosy glow. Banners and shields hung from the walls, silver dishes and real glass beakers graced the high table and every man seemed to be dressed like a chieftain. The hall was crammed to bursting point – noisy, smoky, flowing with ale, and smelling of hot bread and roast pork. Thralls ran to and fro with jugs and platters, men laughed and shouted to each other and the air was thick with humour and good fellowship.

And it was all to honour him! It's as if I'd died and gone to Valhalla, Sigfrid thought blissfully. From his place at his father's side, he looked across the central hearth to where Olaf sat among his own followers. The Norwegian smiled and raised a cup to him and Sigfrid thought his heart would burst with pride. He lifted his own beaker and felt the ale run down into his belly, then up to his head in a warm, muzzy glow.

Olaf's son was not in the hall tonight – too young, so Ivar said, for such occasions – and neither was the boy's mother. Instead, Olaf had at his side a man whom Sigfrid had not yet met. He wasn't sure he wanted to meet him. The man was dark and dour and sat like a curse inflicted on the company. He did not smile or speak, only looked around the hall with baleful eyes and scowled into his drink, as if he suspected someone had dropped cow dung in it.

Sigfrid nudged his father. 'Who is the angry wolf sitting next to Olaf?'

Ivar chuckled. 'That,' he said grimly, 'is our friend Audgils. He has only been here a few weeks. He is kin to Olaf, and they hate each other.'

'So anyone can see. But, why?'

'There is blood between them.'

'Blood!'

'Yes, Audgils was foster son to King Harald of Agdir.'

'So?' Sigfrid tried to remember what he knew of King Harald.

His father explained: 'Harald had a daughter, Asa, who was reputed to be very beautiful. When Olaf's father, Guthroth, was widowed, he took a fancy to Asa and asked Harald for her hand in marriage, but Harald refused him. Guthroth decided if he couldn't have her legally he'd have her by force. He raised a warband and invaded Agdir. It was a bloody business. Harald was killed along with most of his sons, and the bride was carried off. Audgils has never forgiven Olaf's father for the death of Harald and the shaming of his foster-sister. The families have been at blood-feud ever since.'

A blood-feud! Sigfrid caught his breath. This was the stuff sagas were made of. Nothing like that ever happened where he came from. 'And yet Asa continues to live with Guthroth!' he said, shaking his head. 'I wonder she has not put a knife in his back.'

Ivar laughed. 'She probably will one day. But she has a son by him and she has to think of the boy's future. He is not yet old enough to seize power and she wouldn't want to make Olaf a present of the kingdom.'

That made sense. 'She must pray every night that the Valkyries will carry Olaf off in battle over here,' Sigfrid chuckled. A sudden thought struck him. 'Do you suppose that is why Audgils is here? Do you suppose Asa sent him to kill Olaf?'

'It is possible. But I think the man is simply an adventurer with an eye to anything he can grab. He calls himself a king's son and already he is demanding a share in the leadership of Dublin.'

'Will he get it?'

Ivar snorted. 'He can carve himself a slice of Olaf's power if he wants, but there will be blood spilt if he sharpens his knife for mine.'

Sigfrid could believe it. He looked admiringly at his father. Ivar was not tall, but he was built like a menhir and, with fifteen years of fighting experience behind him, it would take an incredibly brave, or foolish, man to cross him. He wondered whether Audgils had the wit to realise that.

The next few weeks passed in a whirlwind of exciting experiences for Sigfrid. Dublin was like nothing he had ever known – a purely masculine world, noisy and dirty, dedicated to the industries of war and thrumming like a bowstring with undercurrents of rivalry and bravado. It was a warrior society, and it existed to serve the ships, the strong, sleek, exquisitely beautiful craft riding at anchor or beached around the shores of the Liffey and the *Dubh Linn*, the black pool which gave the place its name.

Sigfrid loved the ships with a passion he could not put into words. There was a beauty in their lines that satisfied his eye, an aura of menace that fuelled his thirst for adventure. He spent hours watching them glide in and out of the pool, and dreamed of the day when he too would own one. *Storm-Rider*, he would call her and he could already see her in his mind.

For a time, life seemed perfect, but inevitably the novelty wore off. Life in a Viking stronghold was not all feasting and fighting, he discovered. There were still chores to be done and orders to be obeyed. And then there was sword practice. Ivar had instructed Arne to teach Sigfrid all he knew of the art of fighting and the big Viking took his job seriously. Each day he drilled Sigfrid in the use of sword and shield, pushing him until he stumbled from exhaustion and then driving him to his feet to fight some more.

'There's no rest in battle,' he would say grimly, as his pupil struggled and gasped for breath. 'The last man standing wins. Now, shield up again. Strike and block, strike and block. Harder! Put some guts into it! Crowd me. Don't give me room to swing. Keep your arm up or I'll come in over the top of you – like this.' And he would demonstrate, with a flat-bladed wallop that wrenched the boy's weapon from his fist and frequently knocked him off his feet.

Whenever this happened the audience that had inevitably gathered to watch would hoot and laugh and make ribald comments on Sigfrid's prowess. Then he would lose his temper and lash out at Arne in a volley of wild and ill-judged lunges that never came anywhere near their target. Arne would hold him off, chiding remorselessly. 'Shield up. Control your rage, let it work *for* you, not against you. Watch me, anticipate. Use your brain, boy, that's what it's there for.' And so the torture would continue until red mists swam before Sigfrid's eyes and Arne finally judged that he could take no more.

There were days when Sigfrid hated Arne Brodirsson, nights when he lay on his pallet, aching in every muscle, and half wished the past undone and himself safely back in Denmark. They soon passed though, and he never asked for respite. He was Sigfrid Ivarsson, son of the greatest warrior-king of the western seas. One day he too would be a warrior. He would give a man to Odin and know the meaning of victory. And if this was what it took, then so be it. He could bear it. He was a Viking.

And slowly things did improve. His muscles hardened, his body accustomed itself to the punishing exercise, and he grew cunning, learning to fight with his mind as well as his arm. Before long he was beating many of the younger men and even pressing Arne every now and then. Arne acknowledged his progress. He was as generous with his praise as with his criticism, and Sigfrid began to revel in his new-found skills.

All he needed now was an opportunity to use them. He was growing restless. When he had dreamed of the Viking life, he had imagined ... well, he was not sure exactly what he had imagined, but certainly not the long days of boredom and inactivity that seemed to be the pattern of life in Dublin. Weapons had to be forged, boats needed careening, defensive ramparts had to be maintained and repaired. He could understand all that, but where was the adventure he had dreamed of – the fighting, the lightning raids along the coast, the desperate hand-to-hand struggles that would bring him fame and riches and immortality in the mouths of the skalds?

He complained to Arne, but Arne only laughed. 'You'll have your fill of fighting before the year is out,' he promised. 'But raiders need a safe base to return to, and we are not in Denmark here. This is a hostile country. Besides, Dublin is more than a camp now, it is becoming a market.

You cannot eat gold or prisoners, you need to sell them, and merchants won't risk their vessels in an unsafe port.'

'But surely we should be safe here, of all places,' protested Sigfrid. 'After all, the High King of Ireland is Olaf's father-in-law.'

Arne laughed again. 'Ah, Sigfrid, you still have much to learn. Olaf changes wives as frequently as most men change their shirts, and besides, when he married Aed Findliath's daughter, Aed was not the High King but only the *tánaiste*, or expected heir to the previous king, Maolseachlainn.'

'What difference would that make?'

'The Irish have some strange customs. Their High King and his *tánaiste* are traditionally enemies. The title alternates between two branches of the same family and I think both sides fear if they do not prove their strength their branch will be excluded.'

'Ah,' said Sigfrid, beginning to understand. 'So while Maolseachlainn was High King, Aed Findliath needed our help to oppose him, but now ...'

'Now he must turn on us to show his people he can defend them. Already his nephew, Flann mac Connaing of Brega, who was one of our staunchest allies, has turned his back on us and carried his sword to his uncle. I think before the summer is out your father and Olaf will lead a warband into Brega to teach him manners.'

A warband to march aginst Flann mac Connaing! Were these the 'important matters' Olaf had wanted to discuss with his father on the day of their first meeting? Sigfrid felt a prickle of excitement run down his spine. He slept that night with his sword under his pallet and dreamed of honour and glory and the man he would one day give to Odin.

3

THE RAVEN RESTS

'Empty!' spat Olaf, 'just like all the others.' He raised his torch and the light beam swooped in a vicious arc around the interior of the ancient burial chamber. It set grotesque shadows leaping across the vaulted ceiling and made rainbows on the runnels of water trickling down the walls. Sigfrid shivered. There was something malevolent about this place; it was cold and dank and smelt of long centuries of decay. He glanced at his father and saw that Ivar shared his uneasiness. They all turned to look at the fourth member of their group – the man who had led them here.

'Well, Lorcan,' said Ivar, with a mirthless grin, 'so much for the treasures of your ancient gods. I think I prefer your White Christ. He may be less heroic, but his temples are a good deal more profitable.'

Lorcan mac Cashel, King of Mide, shuffled his feet and glanced nervously around the desecrated vault. He is nervous too, thought Sigfrid. To him, this is a sacred place. Despite his White Christ, he still fears the anger of his old Gods.

'Ah well,' said Lorcan, the casual tone of his voice deceiving no one, 'it was worth a try, and it will certainly have taught Flann mac Connaing, and all of Brega, a lesson they'll not forget in a hurry.'

'Indeed it has, and what a great consolation that will be to my warband who were promised gold!' Ivar swung on his heel. 'Faugh! This place has the stink of death about it.' And he ducked into the long, sloping passage that led back to the outside world.

The others followed him. As Sigfrid emerged into the sunlight, he heard Lorcan's voice from behind him, its tone bitter and accusing. 'Gold for your warriors, is it? And where will you be finding that now, Viking, if not in the places of the dead? The homes of the living you have stripped already.'

Ivar didn't answer, but the words rang uncomfortably in Sigfrid's ears. Could the Irishman be right? The raid into Brega had been ruthlessly thorough, but it had unearthed little in the way of plunder and barely a handful of saleable captives. In Dublin he had heard men laughingly refer to Ireland as their 'milk cow', but what would happen if the cow went dry? No man would fight for nothing.

He tried to push the thought from his mind, but it kept coming back and took the edge off his pleasure later that evening as he sat in Lorcan's hall listening to Olaf and Audgils quarrelling.

The two men had been drinking and their raised voices beat against the murmur of conversation like angry fists. Sigfrid wondered what the argument was about this time and whether someone would make a move to stop them before it got out of hand.

In the end it was Ivar who lost his patience. He rose to his feet and slammed his drinking horn down with a roar. 'Gods of chaos, I've had a bellyful of this bickering! If there is blood between you then take it to a holm-gang and make an end to it. And let the rest of us drink our ale in peace.'

A holm gang – the traditional, one-on-one fight to the death to settle a blood feud? Had things really gone that far?

Olaf and Audgils both turned to look at Ivar, then Olaf laughed and leered across the table at his kinsman. 'Well,

Audgils, you heard what the Danish King said. Shall we find an island and fight it out man-to-man, or was it in your mind to put a knife between my shoulder blades some dark night?'

'Fenrir take you, Olaf Guthrothsson, I have killed men for less than that.'

'For insulting your honour? Hah, no man could do that, for it is well known that you have none.'

'Lie-monger!'

'Dung-raker!'

'By the Lord Odin!' Audgils lurched to his feet, over-turning the table in his fury. Food and ale flew in all directions and startled drinkers scrambled for cover, gleeful at the prospect of a fight. Both men now had knives in their hands. Audgils made a clumsy lunge at Olaf, but in his drunkenness he stumbled and sprawled heavily amongst the debris on the floor. A couple of his men hauled him to his feet and put the knife back in his fist. He lurched forward a few paces and he and Olaf began to circle each other, jabbing ineffectively and swaying to and fro on drunken feet.

Olaf, slightly the more sober of the two, began to bait his rival. He flicked the knife back and forth in front of Audgils's face, goading him with mocking encourage-ment. 'Come at me, then. Show me your courage. Show me your skill with the blade. Show me how your foster father fought when my father took his daughter from him.'

'Thrall's get! Murdering son of a sow!' Audgils lunged blindly at his tormentor, and Olaf sidestepped to dodge the blow. The movement threw him off balance. He staggered, flung out his hands to steady himself and toppled backwards into the arms of his supporters. Audgils, pitched forward by the momentum of his swing, stumbled also. He crashed to the ground and lay sprawled there, face downwards among the rushes.

Lorcan pushed his way through the crowd and came to stand between them. He planted one foot on Audgils's back, and drawing his sword brought the point to rest against Olaf's chest. 'Enough,' he ordered.

Olaf blinked at him stupidly. Audgils began to snore. The king of Mide looked down at him in disgust. 'Take him out and put him to bed,' he commanded. 'And you, Olaf of Dublin, remember you are a guest in my hall. For the rest of you, let any other man abuse my hospitality tonight and he will not live long enough to regret it.'

Audgils's companions muttered among themselves. One or two even reached for their knives. But they soon thought better of it. Lorcan's bodyguards were fully armed, but everyone else had been obliged to leave their swords at the door. In the end, a couple of men dragged their still snoring leader back to his quarters and the rest returned to their drinking.

Sigfrid let his breath out in a long sigh. He didn't know whether he was relieved or disappointed. A fight to the death would have been interesting to see, but he had the feeling it was something the leadership of Dublin could ill afford at present. He glanced at his father. Ivar's face had taken on its granite mask. It was impossible to know what he was thinking. Did he support Olaf, or was he hoping the two rivals would finish each other off and leave him in sole possession of the field?

It was several days later before Sigfrid summoned up the courage to ask him. Ivar was brutally frank. 'Olaf and I have been allies for ten years now,' he said. 'But two kings ruling one kingdom can never be close friends. And our very success works against us. As our wealth has grown, so too have the numbers seeking a share of it. Every tide brings new ships to Dublin, and every man on every ship has the same dream. How many times can you keep plundering the same monasteries?'

'So the milk cow really is going dry?'

'No, she just hasn't enough teats for all who are trying to milk her. And now, to add to our troubles, we have this power struggle at the very top.'

'Olaf and Audgils, you mean.'

'And Olaf's son, Eysteinn, and you and ...'

'Me? But I do not plan to challenge anyone.'

'Maybe not. But you are here. Olaf feels threatened, and a man pushed into a corner is dangerous.'

'You think I should not have come?'

'No. You are my son. You have a right to be here and I am proud to acknowledge you. All I am saying is, walk carefully. Do nothing to anger Olaf or Audgils and make sure you never get dragged into their quarrels.'

'You think Olaf will kill him?'

'I think one will kill the other, sooner or later. And I think also that if we wish to preserve our alliance, Olaf and I may have to part company, for a while at least. It is too late now to make any plans for this year, but once winter has come and gone ... well, we shall see what the springtime brings.'

His first winter in Dublin was nothing like the ones Sigfrid had known in Scandinavia, but by Irish standards it was a hard one. The river froze and the longships lay like beached whales along the shores of the *Dubh Linn*. Roads out of the settlement were blocked by snow and travel became almost impossible.

At first it was a novelty. The men carved skates for themselves out of deer antlers. They devised sledge races and formed teams to pelt each other with snowballs or belt a stone around the ice with sticks, but gradually, as the short, cold days dragged on, they lost interest in these pastimes. Bored with each other's company and restless

46

from lack of exercise, they began to do what men frequently do under such circumstances, drink and quarrel.

Fights sprang up out of nowhere. Some men had brought wives over from Norway or Denmark, others, like Guthrum, had taken Irish slave women into their houses, but many ships' companies lived a communal bachelor existence and arguments over women became common. Other men gambled away prize possessions in drunken board games, then tried to reclaim them once they had sobered up. There were constant accusations of theft and cheating. Every insult, every jealousy, every petty grievance, was magnified out of all proportion. The two kings struggled to maintain discipline and harsh penalties were invoked for public brawling. But still the fights broke out. And, through it all, Olaf and Audgils stalked each other like a pair of stags, looking for any weakness they could exploit.

Sigfrid took his father's advice and kept well out of their way. He had other interests. Arne had offered to take him into his crew and teach him all he needed to know in preparation for the time he would own his own ship. Sigfrid was elated. He had huge respect for the big Viking and, short of commanding his own craft, crewing for Arne was the greatest honour he could think of.

He determined to make himself a useful crew member, and it was on an errand for Arne – to fetch an adze inadvertently left on board after a day of working on *Seasnake* – that he came down to the *Dubh Linn* one evening in February, just as darkness was falling. The shoreline looked eerily different in the fading light, remote and grey, a landscape out of Niflheim. Away to the south, the distant mountains loomed like an army of waiting frost-giants. A few gulls still wheeled above the darkening water, a lone oystercatcher fossicked among the rocks, and the beached ships lay like dead whales washed up on the sand. A fire flickered in the lee of one craft and a group of men sat around it drinking, but everyone else had gone home or up to the hall for the evening meal.

Sigfrid shivered as he scrambled onto the sloping deck of the beached *Seasnake*. He had never feared the dark before, but something felt not right about this place tonight, something he could not name and would probably laugh at in the morning. He felt an urgency to be away and back in the brightness of the hall. He found the adze still lying where Arne had said it would be and, with a sigh of relief, picked it up.

As he stood up, a figure detached itself from the group around the fire and came towards him. Sigfrid hesitated. Half his mind urged him to run, the other half said: Don't be absurd. What could there be to fear? Before he could decide, the man was standing in front of him, blocking his path. When he saw who it was, Sigfrid wished he had run.

Audgils stood like a rock, feet apart, hands on his hips, and smiled, as a cat might smile at a mouse. 'Well, well,' he said. 'If it isn't Sigfrid Ivarsswhelp. And what takes a little puppy dog so far from his kennel on such a night? Were you sent to spy on me?'

'No,' said Sigfrid, trying to sound defiant. 'Arne sent me to fetch this.' He held up the adze.

'Did he now? Arne should know better. That's a dangerous toy for a little boy.' In one sudden explosive movement Audgils's hand shot out and wrenched the axe-like tool from Sigfrid's grip. 'You could have a nasty accident with that,' he continued, holding it in front of the boy's face and running a finger down the blade. 'One misplaced footstep, one stumble in the dark … and nobody around to see you fall. What would the king of Dublin say if his son was found here in the morning, with Arne Brodirsson's adze embedded in his skull?'

Sigfrid gulped and backed away. Audgils followed him. 'Little boys should not interfere in men's affairs. Life is a battlefield. Only the strongest survive. How many men do you think I have killed?'

'Not as many as I have,' said a voice behind him. Arne Brodirsson materialised out of the darkness, a drawn sword in his hand. Sigfrid thought he must be dreaming. 'Save your bragging for the hall, Audgils,' the big Viking continued. 'There is nobody to applaud you here.' And before the astonished Norwegian could collect his wits, Arne had stepped forward, whisked the adze out of the man's grasp and stuck it in his own belt. He grinned at Sigfrid. 'Right, young Sigfrid, let's get you back to the hall, your supper is waiting for you. And, the next time I send you on an errand, don't make me have to come looking for you.'

He put a casual arm across his protégé's shoulder and steered him up the beach and towards the town. Not once did he bother to glance around to see if Audgils was following. Sigfrid could hardly believe such confidence. 'How did you know?' he demanded, once they were back in the safety of the settlement. 'How did you know I was in trouble?'

'I didn't,' grinned his rescuer. 'But I had seen Audgils down by the pool earlier, and when you were slow returning, I began to worry.'

Sigfrid shivered. 'Was he ... would he really ... ?'

'I don't know. Probably not. I think he just wanted to frighten you.' Arne stopped and looked at him. 'It is in my mind that it would be better not to speak of this to your father. He would want to kill Audgils, and that would only cause more conflict. Leave the fool to sweat it out and wonder. He'll never be certain now who knows and who doesn't and he'll spend the rest of his life looking over his shoulder.'

Sigfrid agreed, but he promised himself that from now on he was going to stick to Arne's side like caulking to a ship.

Eventually, to everyone's relief, the winter came to an end, and somehow, through luck or the intervention of the Gods, both Olaf and Audgils had managed to survive. The warmer weather brought a new sense of purpose to the settlement. Many men had grown weary of Dublin and the first spring tides saw an exodus of disillusioned boat crews. The traffic was not all one way, however, and one day Sigfrid was summoned to the hall to be introduced to two newcomers: Ivar's brothers Ubbe and Halfdan.

Sigfrid liked his uncles right away. Halfdan was a big man, full of restless energy – a warrior, cast in the same mould as Olaf Guthrothsson. Ubbe was slighter, quieter, more self-contained. His eyes were the same sea-storm grey as Ivar's and they had a way of gazing off into the distance as if they saw things other men could not. Both men had spent the previous year raiding in the land of the Franks. Halfdan, in particular, was not impressed by the domesticity he found in Dublin. 'You grow soft here, brother,' he told Ivar. 'The ice is gone from the rivers, the last of the snows has melted, and still your ships lie beached in the harbour like a colony of breeding seals. Has the Irish climate so thinned your blood you forget the Viking life?'

'I have obligations,' protested Ivar. 'A kingdom to defend and ...'

'A kingdom! Loki's beard, when did a sea-wolf ever need a kingdom? A ship is all the realm a Viking needs.' Halfdan waved an angry hand at the banner over the high seat. 'Look at it. Our father's banner – the raven of Ragnar Lodbrok. Was it made to hang limply from the wall of an Irish mead hall?'

'He speaks the truth, brother,' agreed Ubbe. 'It is hungry. Give it wings, let it feast again.'

Ivar laughed, but his eyes were very dark. Sigfrid guessed what was going through his mind. His dreams of conquering Ireland were no closer to fulfilment now than they had ever been. Dublin had become just one more square in the patchwork of Irish politics, and alliances were a waste of time in a country where men changed their loyalties as cheerfully as they changed their wives. 'We shall see what the springtime brings,' he had said and now it had brought his brothers. Was it Odin's wind had blown their ships into the *Dubh Linn*?

'So,' Ivar said at last, softly, 'you would have me follow the whale-road again. But where shall we go? Where would you have my raven feed?'

Halfdan and Ubbe exchanged glances. 'Have you heard men speak of the holy island?' asked Halfdan.

'Holy island!' Ivar spluttered into his ale. 'Fafnir's blood, Halfdan, this country is infested with holy islands and at one time or another we've plundered every one of them!'

'Nay then, it is not Ireland I am talking of. This island lies off the northeast coast of England, in the kingdom of Northumbria. The monks who live there call it Lindisfarne.'

'Monks?' Ivar's ears pricked up.

'Bjarni Sigurdsson, my helmsman, told me of it. He said that many years ago a raiding party of Norwegians came on it by chance and carried off more gold and treasures than you could ever dream of.'

'Then doubtless others will have raided it since and sucked it dry. Besides, one monastery would not sustain us for long. Between us we must number nearly two hundred ships.'

'Where there is one there will be more,' said Halfdan stubbornly. Bjarni says Northumbria is ripe with wealth.'

'And all of it stoutly defended, no doubt.'

'Nay then, if he speaks truly, the warriors of Northumbria are too busy fighting among themselves to repel invaders. They have deposed their king and put a usurper in his place and the whole country is in turmoil. I tell you there is a fortune there for the taking and ...' Halfdan broke off and glanced shrewdly at his brother, 'and maybe a kingdom too, to pass on to your son, one he will not have to share with Eysteinn Olafsson.'

'But I ...' Sigfrid opened his mouth to say again that he did not want a kingdom, then changed his mind. His father was not listening. He was staring with far-away eyes into the ashes of the fire, hearing the old sword song again.

'We would have to move cautiously,' said Ivar at last. 'An armed kingdom, even one at war with itself, would be no easy prize. We would need to winter further south and spy out the land. And we would need food and horses.'

'Bjarni says ...'

'He seems to say a good deal, this Bjarni Sigurdsson. Where does he come by all this information? Is he to be trusted?'

'Bjarni has been trading, and raiding, around the coasts of England for years, and his father before him. There is not a river or an estuary he does not know. He says there is a kingdom to the south of Northumbria where they raise the best barley and the best horses in England, a land where rivers cross the countryside like roads and ships can find safe harbour among the islands in the marshes. He says it would make ideal winter quarters.'

'He seems to have thought of everything,' said Ivar dryly. He frowned and stared deeper into the fire. Half-dan and Ubbe watched him anxiously. Sigfrid held his breath. Finally Ivar lifted his head. A grim smile settled across his face. 'This land of rivers and marshes,' he asked softly, 'what name do they give to it?'

Sigfrid knew the argument was won. Halfdan grinned at Ubbe, drained his cup and sent it spinning across the room to shatter triumphantly against the hearthstones.

'They call it East Anglia,' he said.

4

TAKING THE WHALE'S ROAD

They were going a-viking – not just a raiding expedition, but a full-scale seaborne invasion of the Anglian kingdoms. Sigfrid could hardly contain his excitement. This was real adventure. This was what he had come to Dublin to find. It seemed the whole settlement felt the same way. The place thrummed with anticipation and the shores of the black pool had become the focus of frenzied activity. New ships were being built, old ones recaulked and floated. Ropemakers, sailmakers, coopers and shipwrights were working as though their lives depended on it, and the anvil in the smithy rang from dawn to dusk as weapons were manufactured or repaired. Boat crews working on their vessels drew together into tightly bonded groups, and this time he was one of them, part of the fellowship of Arne Brodirsson's *Seasnake*. The dream he had cherished all his life was finally coming true.

Sigfrid imagined the fame he would earn, the treasures he would win, and he watched in admiration as his father supervised the preparations. Ivar worked tirelessly, planning, issuing orders, settling disputes. Like a master ropemaker, he gathered into his hands all the separate strands of activity and plaited them into one single, solid cord. This campaign had given him a new sense of purpose. He looked taller, younger, infused with the old Viking spirit.

Sigfrid had wondered what Olaf would say when he learned of their plans. But the Norwegian seemed, if anything, relieved. 'There is little enough for anyone here in Dublin at the moment,' he agreed when Ivar explained his reasons. 'I have half a mind to take the whale's road again myself.'

'Have you so?' Ivar sounded suspicious. 'And where would you plan to feed *your* ravens?'

Olaf laughed. 'Nay, I'll not come treading on your toes. There are pickings enough further north for my warriors. Constantine mac Cinnead, King of the Scots, is locked in conflict with the Picts and,' he lowered his voice to a conspiratorial whisper, 'he has offered me one of his sisters in return for my support.'

'Ha!' Ivar spluttered with mirth. 'I should have known there would be a woman in it somewhere. How many wives will that make? Three?'

'Four,' said Olaf carelessly. 'I left one behind in Vestfold too.'

'So. And what will the Irish High King say when he learns you have abandoned his daughter for a Scottish princess?'

Olaf shrugged. 'Let him say what he will. Audgils can deal with him.'

'Audgils?'

'He wanted Dublin, didn't he? Let him have it then. He can sit here and pretend to be king, until we return.'

'Ah, but will he be content here? If he really is pursuing a blood-feud, he may decide to follow you.'

'Then he will wish he hadn't. Audgils is all belly and no guts. I can settle with him any time I choose.' Olaf dismissed his rival with a careless laugh and Sigfrid envied him his confidence. He wondered how Olaf would have fared that night down by the ships.

The Norwegian clapped them both on the back. 'Good luck to your seafaring, Ivar Ragnarsson, and you also, young Sigfrid. May Odin send you a helm wind, and bring you safe landfall in Dublin again when your voyaging is done.'

'We will keep in touch,' said Ivar. 'And may Constantine's sister be as beautiful and obedient as her brother has doubtlessly boasted her to be.'

'Will Audgils really follow him, do you think?' asked Sigfrid when he and his father were alone again.

'More than likely,' said Ivar. 'It is in my mind we have not heard the last of that conflict. But Olaf can look after himself. He has not lived this long without learning a trick or two. Anyway, I have problems enough of my own without making fosterlings of his.'

When preparations for the voyage were almost completed, Ivar sought counsel of the Gods before making his final plans. A thrall – the strongest, best-looking young man they could find – was hanged in sacrifice to Odin. Beneath the gallows, Ubbe cast the runes. Sigfrid watched the ceremony in awe. The runes, he knew, were the highest of all magic and few men dared to invoke their power. Odin himself had won the secret of their symbols after hanging for nine days on the tree of life. Which was why runemasters liked to offer a victim on the gallows before casting the runes themselves.

Ubbe was skilled in his art. He sat for a long time, studying the small, inscribed squares of birch bark. Then he touched each one in turn and explained its significance to his audience. 'The omens are good,' he told his watchers. 'Odin smiles on us. See, here are the runes of success and victory. But the all-father demands payment for his help. In return for his favour he commands that we dedicate our victory to him in the highest form possible.'

'King-sacrifice!' Ivar and Halfdan breathed the word simultaneously. Sigfrid saw the look that passed between them. Ivar stood up. He drew his sword and, with both hands, he raised it high above his head. His eyes were as bright and fierce as the sun that glinted off the blade. 'Hear me, Odin,' he called, and his voice rolled across the settlement like the blast of a war horn. 'Hear me, Odin, God of battles, this I swear to you: put into my hands the king of Northumbria, and I myself will carve the blood-eagle on his back and give him to you for victory.'

Sigfrid felt a shiver run down his spine. He was left speechless, not so much by the words as by their intensity. Hoskuld, sacrificing his horses to Freyr, had never displayed this kind of fervour. What had given Ivar this devotion to Odin? Sigfrid's own feelings towards the enigmatic, one-eyed God had always been somewhat mixed. Thor was more his idea of a Viking God. Big, bluff, uncomplicated – an Olaf Guthrothsson sort of a fellow – you knew where you stood with Thor. Odin was devious and not totally to be trusted.

It puzzled him, but then ... Why, of course, they are

two of a kind, he thought. Ivar and Odin, Olaf and Thor; there was a balance there. It was probably why the two kings had been so successful in partnership. And Ivar had been raiding and fighting for more than fifteen years now. Somebody must have been looking out for him.

Later he told Arne what he had seen. Arne was impressed. 'Your father has always followed Odin,' he said. 'After every battle he offers him sacrifice. He believes the all-father has singled him out for greatness, and he may well be right. But the bloodeagle, eh?' He gave a short whistle. 'Now there is a promise never lightly made. I wish I had been there to hear it.'

'It was ...' Sigfrid faltered. It was difficult to describe the impression Ivar had made, standing beneath the gallows 'He looked ...' Sigfrid gave up. 'But what is the bloodeagle, Arne?'

'You have never seen it? No, I was forgetting, you were not here when we sacrificed the king of Munster. It is the most solemn of all rituals, the noblest of victims, sent to Odin on the wings of the king of birds.'

'Yes, but what *is* it? What actually happens?'

'The victim's body is made to look like an eagle in flight. His ribs are cut away from the backbone, like this,' Arne ran two fingers down Sigfrid's back, on either side of his spine. 'Then they are pulled apart and the lungs are lifted out – still attached – to flutter like wings as he draws his last few breaths.'

'Hel's teeth!' Sigfrid tried to imagine it. He remembered what Ivar had said to him about giving a man to Odin at the point of your sword. Suddenly the words took on a whole new significance.

The day came for their departure. Under the gaze of almost everyone still left in Dublin, the Danish ships, their sails broad and fatbellied with wind, streamed out of the mouth of the Poddle like a pride of dragons. Warriors in full battle harness lined their decks, walls of overlapping shields decorated their sides, and on the foremost vessel, the raven of Ragnar Lodbrok soared in triumph from the mast. It was a spectacle Sigfrid knew he would never forget. As he stood among his fellow crewmen on the deck of *Seasnake*, waving to the well-wishers on the shore, he thought his heart would burst with pride. For the first time in his life he wore full battle harness. A tunic of boiled leather covered his chest and loins, a magnificent sheepskin cloak hung from his shoulders, pinned with a silver brooch. His sword – Hoskuld's sword – burnished and honed to a fine edge, swung proudly at his hip and on his head was a gilded helmet, a present from his father. He looked at the new dragon-head snarling from *Seasnake's* prow and felt like a hero out of legend.

Since they were planning to winter in East Anglia, Sigfrid had assumed they would sail directly there, but the runes had dictated otherwise. Patience and cunning, they had advised, and Ivar was a past master in both arts. He set up a base on the island of Thanet, and from there spent the summer raiding the southern coast of England, toughening his crews, whetting their appetite for plunder and sharpening their skills for the task that lay ahead. He also made more long-term plans. Ubbe was dispatched with his ships to Northumbria to make contact with the deposed king, Osbert. 'Offer him your services to help him oust his rival,' ordered Ivar. 'If you can win his trust and install your warband in his country, then by the time we join you next year, half our battle will be won.'

Ubbe chuckled. 'We shall be invincible,' he promised. 'With your cunning, Halfdan's strength and my skill with the runes, who can stand against us? I shall send word as soon as I have secured my position.'

With his brother gone, Ivar set about securing his own winter quarters. Bjarni Sigurdsson had spoken truly when he talked of rivers crossing the land like roads. The fens and mudflats of East Anglia could have been designed for Viking ships and under Bjarni's guidance the marauders moved with devastating swiftness. From Aldeburgh to the Norfolk Broads the land went up in flames as they swept through the coastal marshes, leaving behind them plundered villages, ruined harvests and a countryside reeking with the smoke of their brutality. Finally they drove inland, up the Waveney. Near Hoxne they turned briefly southward on the Dove to plunder the town of Eye. At Redgrave they hauled their ships across the fen to the Little Ouse, and at last, they came to Thetford, where they beached their ships and set about the capture of the town.

The battle for Thetford was Sigfrid's first experience of full-scale warfare, but when it was over he could remember surprisingly little of it. Sounds rather than sights lingered in his memory: shouts, screams, the clash of steel on steel, a dull undulating roar, like the sound of waves on rocks. And, above it all, a voice – his own, he recalled with shock – howling like a hungry wolf.

'You fought like a berserker,' Arne told him approvingly that evening, as they feasted in the blood-spattered moot hall. 'It was as though your sword had taken on a life of its own. And your battle cry – we shall have to call you Sigfrid Wolf-Tongue from now on.'

'You did well,' agreed his father. 'Your first battle, and already your sword has brought you honour. You will have to find a name for it, now you have blooded it.'

Sigfrid glowed with pride. He looked at his blade, trying to think of a suitably impressive title.

'You could call it *RavenFeeder*,' suggested Arne.

Sigfrid shook his head. 'No, too commonplace. Every

second man in this company has a *RavenFeeder*.'

What about *WoundDealer*, then?'

'Or *BloodDrinker*?' offered Ivar.

'No.' Sigfrid frowned and his hand caressed the polished silver hilt. He wanted something more meaningful, something unique, something that would encapsulate all the dreams he had invested in this weapon. He dug deep into his mind and suddenly recalled the name his father had laid on him, in jest, at their first meeting. Of course, the perfect title. He drew the blade from its scabbard and held it out so that firelight caught the metal and burnished it to a golden red. 'I name you *TruthSeeker*,' he said. 'And on your blade I pledge myself to Odin. With you I will give him kings and earls to feed his ravens and earn myself wisdom and undying fame.'

'To Odin, bringer of victories,' intoned Ivar, raising his ale horn.

'To Odin,' echoed the company. And everybody drank.

With the town under his control and his winter quarters secured, Ivar turned his thoughts to the next stage of his campaign. 'We hold the Town Reeve among our prisoners,' he said. 'Bring him here, I wish to question him.'

The man was dragged into the hall and dumped unceremoniously before the high seat. He had been in the thick of the fighting and was in a sorry state, battered and bleeding, scarcely able to stand. Ivar looked at him dispassionately. 'I wish to send a messenger to your king,' he told him. 'I will give you your life and your freedom if you tell me where I can find him.'

'Not here.' The man blinked, only half comprehending. One of the guards struck him across the face with a clenched fist.

'I know he is not here,' Ivar said patiently. 'If he were, I would have no need of you. I ask again, where is he?'

The man shook his head. Again the guard struck him. Something seemed to snap in the prisoner's mind. He began to struggle violently, swearing and shouting and calling down curses on his captors. His East Anglian dialect was close enough to the Vikings' for them to understand most of the abuse. Ivar waited until the man had exhausted himself. 'Take him outside,' he ordered, 'and beat some answers out of him. Let me know as soon as he says anything useful.'

They dragged him out. A long time passed before one of the men came back into the hall.

'Well?' said Ivar.

'Hellesdon, my Lord. The East Anglian king is in his hall at Hellesdon, about half a day's ride north-west of here.'

'You are sure of this?'

'Oh yes, my Lord, very sure.' The man grinned. He

had obviously enjoyed his work.

'Good, then we can make our plans.'

☙ ☙ ☙

The messenger stood before the high seat in the king's hall at Hellesdon. He was a Saxon, the son of a Kentish thane, and he knew it was for that reason, rather than any other, that Ivar had chosen him for his mission. He was a warning, a reminder to his hearers of what might happen if they failed to heed his words. He knew also that there were many here who would consider him a traitor, but he was a practical man. His home was destroyed and his family dead at the hands of a marauding army. It seemed to him more sensible to be marching, a free man, in the ranks of that army, than lying with his throat cut in the ruins of his father's house.

He looked around the hall. The whole East Anglian Witan had assembled to hear him. They were frightened, he could read it in their eyes. The ealdormen shifted uneasily. Bishop Humbert fingered the silver cross around his neck and moved his lips in silent prayer. The messenger felt a glow of self-importance. He was a young man, and like many young men inclined to arrogance. Never before in his life had he wielded this kind of authority or been the focus of such attention. He drew himself up to his full height and launched into the speech he had been rehearsing all the way from Thetford.

'The mighty sea-wolf, Ivar Ragnarsson, fiercest of warriors, conqueror of kings and dealer of wound-gold in all the lands he has invaded, has landed with a great warband on the shores of your kingdom and means to make his winter quarters here. He commands that you surrender to him your lands and wealth and acknowledge him as your overlord. Obey him, and he will allow you to rule this country in his name. Refuse, and ...'

He stopped. For the first time his eyes met those of the man he had been sent to address and suddenly his confidence deserted him. Why had no one warned him that the East Anglian King would be so ... so big? Edmund Alkmundson was built like a yearling bull, as broad, as solid and as good to look at, and probably as dangerous when angered. He was angry now. Every sinew in his body quivered with controlled rage, his eyes were like crystals of blue ice and his fists, clenched on the table in front of him, looked powerful enough to break a man's neck with one blow. The messenger gulped. His fine speech, that had sounded so heroic when he first practised it, was now beginning to seem merely foolish and bombastic. He stammered and took a half step backwards.

The king watched him. 'Refuse and what?' he asked softly.

The messenger opened his mouth and shut it again. It was an agonising while before he could make his voice obey him. 'If ... if you refuse his offer,' he stammered at last, 'th ... then my Lord will consider you unworthy of his mercy and ... and will deal with you accordingly.' It was a pathetic ultimatum, but he no longer had the heart for rhetoric.

There was a long silence. The ice-shard eyes continued to study him as though he were some kind of insect. Finally the king spoke.

'You are not a Scandinavian?'

'N...no, my Lord. West Saxon.'

'So.' Another silence. 'And what am I to do with a West Saxon who takes Viking gold?'

'Hang him,' growled somebody.

'Drown him like a dog in the nearest river,' said someone else. 'Hanging's too good for him.'

The messenger panicked. This wasn't how it was supposed to end. He fell to his knees. 'My Lord, I beg you ... I did not ... I was ordered ... I did not dare refuse.' A sudden inspiration came to him. 'My Lord, I am a prisoner of the Vikings. I was compelled to serve them. But I have no love for them. Ever since my capture I have only been seeking to escape. Give me sanctuary here and ...'

'And spend the rest of my life looking over my shoulder?' Edmund's voice was scathing.

'No, my Lord! I swear I would serve you faithfully.'

'As you have served your own people? Faithful! You do not know the meaning of the word. It is in my mind that you would betray Christ himself for the saving of your skin. You are a coward and a traitor and I should gut you where you grovel.'

The messenger began to weep. He knew it would not aid his cause, but he could not help himself. 'You do not understand,' he snivelled. 'These Vikings, they are so powerful, so merciless. Ah, my Lord, if you knew how I have suffered.'

'I know how Thetford has suffered,' said the king's voice from above him. Do you think I care about your miserable hide? Look at me when I speak to you.'

The messenger lifted his head. The king stared at him with a coldness that turned his bowels to water. 'I should gut you where you grovel,' he repeated, 'but I cannot bring myself to stain my sword with such filthy blood. Get out of here. Go to the kitchens and tell them to feed you. I will take counsel of my Witan, and when we have composed a suitable answer for that heathen pirate you serve, we will summon you again.'

5

THE SQUIRREL OF YGGDRASIL

'Well?' demanded Ivar.

The messenger shuffled his feet. He cast a beseeching glance around his audience and they watched him with varying degrees of amusement and irritation. Sigfrid, who was standing next to Arne in the front row, nudged his mentor in the ribs. 'He looks like a mouse running between two cats,' he whispered. 'But he is a fool not to speak. Can't he see my father is losing his patience?'

'Maybe he's not able to,' chuckled Arne. 'Maybe the East Anglian king cut his tongue out.'

Sigfrid giggled.

'I am waiting,' said Ivar ominously.

The messenger opened and shut his mouth. 'M…my Lord, you must understand, these are not my words. I only repeat what … what … '

His voice trailed off. Ivar set down his beaker of ale. 'I am not interested in your choice of words,' he said with dreadful quietness. 'I am waiting to hear what answer Edmund of East Anglia makes to my demands, and you stand there scuffing your heels and bleating like a castrated bull calf. Are you going to speak or must I thrash it out of you with the end of a rope?'

'No, my Lord! No!' The man shuddered and drew a deep breath. 'King Edmund bids me tell you that he has listened to your terms and finds nothing in them acceptable. He says you can have little understanding of kingship, since you offer him a crown he already wears, his life which, without honour, is worthless to him, and in return you would have him foreswear the sacred oath he took before his people on the day of his coronation.'

Ivar's mouth fell open. 'And did you tell him what would happen if he refused?'

'I did, my Lord.'

'Yet he still defies me?'

The messenger nodded miserably. 'He says he would rather fight for his freedom now, while he still has it, than waste tearful entreaties trying to win it back after he has sold it. He says his stewardship is a sacred trust from God, that he will not, cannot, deliver it into the hands of a pagan, and that if you want East Anglia, then first …' he gulped, 'first you must … '

'Yes?'

'You must become a Christian, my Lord.'

'*What*?' Rage swept Ivar to his feet. His hands slammed down, overturning his ale cup and sending a stream of liquid across the table. 'Gods of chaos! Does he dare to say this? To suggest that I, Ivar of Dublin, son of the great Ragnar Lodbrok, should abandon my Gods and crawl on my belly to his White Christ? By the jaws of Fenrir, he will pay for this arrogance.'

'It is outrageous, my Lord,' the messenger hastened to agree, his courage somewhat restored now that he had delivered his speech. 'I tried my hardest, but what can one do with such a man?'

'Oh, I know what I'll do with him,' said Ivar softly, 'if I ever get my hands on him. So, and did he have any other words of wisdom?'

'Well, yes, my Lord. One final message, but it was a riddle, I think. I did not understand it.'

'And? Speak it, then.'

'He said, "Tell the Lord Ivar he should find himself a more nimble squirrel, lest it come back to him next time with its eyes pecked out."'

'Gods of Asgard!' Ivar's face went from red to purple to white. There was a silence. Then, unexpectedly, he laughed. 'Hel's teeth,' he spluttered when he could speak again. 'So this Saxon puppy has a sense of humour as well as an impertinent tongue. A squirrel, eh? I wonder who told him that story.' He looked down at the bewildered messenger. 'Well, my little Ratatosk, it seems this joke has saved your hide. Be thankful for my laughter and make yourself invisible before my mood changes and I send you back, headless and limbless to the East Anglian king as a warning against insolence.'

The man didn't need telling twice. He fled to his sleeping quarters with the mirth of the camp ringing in his ears.

Once he had left, the assembly soon broke up. Ivar and Halfdan retired to discuss their next move. Arne went off to complete some work on his ship and Sigfrid was left to his own devices. He was bored and there seemed little to do around the camp. He polished *TruthSeeker*, cleaned his battle harness, deloused his shirt and finally, in search of amusement, made his way to the big barn where many of the rank and file of Ivar's warband had their sleeping quarters.

He found the messenger lying on his pallet, looking very sorry for himself. The man scowled when he saw him. 'What do *you* want?' he asked.

Sigfrid grinned. 'Cheer up, Leofric. Look, I've brought you a drink.' He pulled a flask of ale from under his cloak.

Leofric eyed it suspiciously. He scowled again. 'Why would you bring me a drink? What do you want?' he repeated ungraciously.

'Nothing. Just to talk. I'm curious.'

'Then go and talk to your father. He thinks he knows everything. What are you curious about?'

'About the king of the East Anglians.' He sat down on the edge of the mattress and offered Leofric the flask. 'What's he like?'

The Saxon took a long gulp of ale and wiped his mouth with the back of his hand. 'Angry,' he said. 'Big and angry. A beautiful, wrathful, golden giant. He probably eats little boys like you for breakfast!'

Sigfrid flushed indignantly. 'I'm not a little boy. I'm sixteen, and I'm going to have my own ship as soon as we get to Northumbria. I'm not afraid of any Saxon king.'

'No? Then it's a pity your father did not send *you* to carry his messages.'

A picture flashed across Sigfrid's mind. He laughed. 'Poor little Ratatosk. It's a dangerous business being a squirrel.'

'What squirrel? Why does everyone call me Ratatosk?'

'You don't know? You have really never heard of the squirrel of Yggdrasil?'

'Would I be asking if I had?'

'All right then.' Sigfrid settled himself more comfortably on the mattress. 'I'll tell you. But it's a complicated story. I suppose I'd better start with the tree of life. At the centre of the world there stands a mighty ash tree, so huge its branches shade the realms of Gods and men alike. Its name is Yggdrasil. Beneath its roots is the spring of Mimir – the fountain of wisdom and understanding. This spring is very precious and for a single draught of its waters, my Lord Odin once sacrificed one of his eyes.

'Near the tree live the three Norns: Fate, Being and Necessity. It is their job to tend Yggdrasil. Every day they must refresh it with pure water and whiten it with clay from the spring. If they cease to care for it, it will die, for many creatures gnaw at its roots and ...'

'Yes, yes,' broke in Leofric testily, 'it all sounds very beautiful, but what about the squirrel?'

'I'm coming to that part. On the topmost branch of Yggdrasil, there stands an eagle, with a hawk perched on his forehead. At the bottom of the tree lives a snake. The snake and the eagle are at war with each other and they employ a little squirrel called Ratatosk to run up and down the tree carrying insulting messages between them.'

'So.' The messenger was silent for a moment. 'And Edmund of East Anglia compares me to that squirrel.'

'So it would seem. And, since he threatens to peck your eyes out, he must see himself as the eagle and my father as the snake. It is a fine arrogance – but one he may well come to regret.' As he spoke, a memory of the rune-casting flashed across Sigfrid's mind. He recalled his father's vow beneath the gallows. 'We have a special way with kings,' Sigfrid said softly. 'When we catch this Edmund, we shall give him wings and watch him fly to Odin.'

'*When* you catch him?' jeered Leofric. 'You mean *if* you catch him. They are born with webbed feet, these East Anglians. They can disappear into their fens like wild fowl and it would take an army three times the size of your father's to flush them out again.'

Sigfrid laughed, but he was to recall those words often in the weeks that followed.

His father decided to waste no time in handing out a lesson to the brash young East Anglian. Within days of Leofric's return, Ivar personally led a warband to Helles-don – only to find the royal hall abandoned. He had to content himself with burning it to the ground before returning to Thetford. And there a shock awaited him. In his absence, an East Anglian raiding party had slipped through his defences, burned three of his boats and disappeared back into the fens. Edmund had declared war on the invaders.

It was a war that developed into a deadly game of cat and mouse. Ivar burned farms, sacked villages and combed the fens in search of his enemy, but always Edmund stayed one move ahead of him, and, as the days shortened and autumn slipped into winter, the Danish death toll slowly mounted. Boats were ambushed and burned. Search parties chasing an apparently fleeing foe across the marshes were tricked and lured to their death in treacherous bogs. Stories filtered back to Thetford of stragglers from Danish raiding parties caught and flayed alive by the East Anglians and their skins nailed to the doors of churches as an offering to the White Christ.

Worse than all this, however, was the growing problem of supply. Ivar had counted on subjugating East Anglia and commandeering all the food and equipment he needed from a docile countryside; instead he was obliged to waste men and ships in endless raiding expeditions. And there were still his plans for Northumbria. What would happen if he could not obtain horses before next summer? With Ubbe away, he cast the runes again himself, and was comforted to discover they still predicted victory. But they didn't say how and they didn't say when. It was going to be a long, hard winter.

☻ ☻ ☻

Seasnake slid through the moonlit water with the sinuous grace of her namesake. Her dragon-head prow cast a long shadow over the silent reed beds. At his oar, Sigfrid pulled strongly, his eyes fixed on the sweat-stained back of the man in front of him, and dreamed of the day he would be doing this on his own boat.

Already his father had begun to build craft to replace those burnt by the East Anglians and one was going to be his, the *Storm-Rider* of his dreams. Under the supervision of his father's best shipwrights, he was involving himself in every stage of her construction. He had helped to select and fell the massive oak tree from which her keel had been cut. He had split logs and fashioned planks for her strakes and crossbeams. And as he worked on her, or stood and watched her taking shape at the water's edge, he felt for her almost as a man feels for a woman. He had picked his crew: a group of tough, like-minded young men who waited with scarcely less eagerness than himself for the day when she would slide into the water to carry them on exploits of undying glory.

Arne's helmsman raised his arm in a silent order. The rowers shipped their oars and watched as he swung *Seasnake* around by the big rudder on her starboard quarter and ran her up onto the soft mud at the river's edge.

Almost before she grounded, the men had leapt ashore and were hauling her up the bank. When this was done, they brought their weapons and equipment ashore and built a small fire for those who would remain on ship-keep while the raiding party was away. A fire, however small, was a risk, but they were in an isolated spot, their quarry a solitary hall about half a mile away. They would be gone all night, and it was too cold in mid December for men to stand guard in the open without a fire.

When at last all the preparations had been completed, the raiding party moved out silently. Like a pack of hunting wolves they crept through the water meadows along the river's edge, up through long, dark acres of woodland and finally over the brow of a small hill. From here they looked down over frosted ploughland towards the hall. Their information had been correct. The place looked prosperous and undefended. Solid, high-gabled, flanked by its byres and granaries, it slept in the moonlight, snug and unwary as a dreaming dog. It was a prize to tempt any plunder-hungry warband, and it was theirs for the taking, if they were swift and daring enough.

Arne motioned everyone to stillness and Sigfrid felt the hairs on his neck rise and prickle. There was an added danger in a raid like this that made it all the more exciting. The usual pattern in a Viking attack was for several ships to swoop down off the sea on some unsuspecting coastal hamlet, fire its buildings, slaughter its inhabitants and be away with the spoils before help could arrive. But tonight's raid was different. They were a single ship's crew and some way inland. Escape would not be so easy on the river. So tonight there would be no arson and no prisoners. When the killing was over they would strip the hall of everything usable, then spend the night there quietly. At first light they would load their spoils onto ox carts and lead the livestock from their winter byres down to the river where they would be slaughtered.

Sigfrid fingered the hilt of his sword and awaited orders. Down at the hall, a man came out and stood for a moment against the side of the building to relieve himself. The boy watched him with grim amusement. How would the Saxon feel, he mused, if he knew that death was watching him from the top of the hill with twenty pairs of hungry eyes? He wondered how many others there were in the hall and whether they were all asleep.

The man went back inside and shut the door. Arne lifted his hand and the raiders moved forward, creeping down the shadow of the hill. They moved on whisper-quiet feet, so skilled at this stalking game that they were less than a hundred paces from the building before the first dog barked. A man came to the door and peered out into the night, trying to see what the fuss was about. He raised a lantern and called out to the dogs to silence them.

The light framed his figure in a golden glow. Arne ran forward. His arm swung, his axe sang through the air and took the man full in the chest. The Saxon dropped like a stone, and, howling like the hordes of Hel, the Vikings swept out of the shadows and in through the open doorway.

The struggle was short and bloody. The Saxons, startled out of sleep by the attack, were no match for their assailants. To Sigfrid, the killing seemed to happen in a crimson dream. He saw nothing clearly. The opposition had congealed into a single mass of arms and weapons. He hacked and thrust in an orgy of destruction and his voice came back to him, roaring and howling like a berserker.

Finally the frenzy was over. Panting like a spent animal, Sigfrid leaned on his sword and looked about him at the carnage he had helped to create. The place was a shambles. Tables were overturned, benches broken, pottery smashed. Corpses lay everywhere, sprawled in the obscenity of death, and Arne's men were going around finishing off any who still breathed. He looked down at his reeking blade. How many men had it killed? What had they felt as the cold steel entered their bodies? Had they seen death written in his eyes? He wished he could remember, but he had no sense of individual victory. It was all so impersonal. How could you look into a man's eyes when your own must always watch his weapon hand?

When the last of the Saxon bodies had been stripped and dragged outside for the wolves and ravens to find, the Vikings began to gather their booty. Some went to ransack the kitchen while others were dispatched to search the outbuildings. Arne pointed out to Sigfrid a manhole leading to a loft above the roof beams. 'Find a ladder and see what's up there,' he told the boy. 'If there is any hay or straw, throw some down to mop up this mess on the floor.'

Arming himself with a lighted torch, Sigfrid did as he was told. The loft was small and appeared to contain nothing but stooks of hay and straw. He kicked several of them down through the manhole and was about to descend when his torch caught the glint of something half hidden in the thatch. He pulled it out and saw that it was a flagon, sealed with a plug of wax.

Why would anyone have hidden such a thing, he wondered? He cut away the plug with his dagger and sniffed the contents. Then he understood. Wine, and a very special wine, by the smell of it. He put the flagon to his lips and the smooth liquid trickled down his throat like nectar. This was a prize indeed, somebody's secret treasure, hidden away to be savoured in selfish solitude. Well, whoever had owned it certainly wouldn't be wanting it now. It was his, and there was no way he was going to add it to the common hoard. Tucking it back into its hiding place, he climbed out of the loft and moved the ladder to discourage anyone else from exploring.

In the hall the celebrations had already started. Arne had shared out a portion of the spoils from the kitchen and he and his crew sat around the central hearth, joking and laughing, with bread and chunks of smoked mutton in their hands and ale jugs at their sides. Some were already well into their cups and it did not take Sigfrid long to catch up with them. Replete with food and pleasantly drunk, he lounged among the rushes on the floor, listening sleepily while Arne played a plundered harp and sang them the tale of Sigurd Dragonslayer.

Sigfrid liked the Volsung legend. It reminded him of his grandfather, Ragnar Lodbrok, for Ragnar was also said to have killed a dragon in his youth. He swelled with pride as he thought about it. How many men in this room could boast a dragonslayer for a grandfather?

The night wore on and some of the heavier drinkers began to fall asleep around the fire. Sigfrid yawned and thought of his wine. A mouthful or two before sleep would put a final glow on the night's adventures; also the loft with its sheaves of straw would make a warm bedchamber. Stumbling a little, he climbed back up the ladder and pulled it up behind him, so no one could intrude on his solitude. He uncorked the wine flagon, and it was so good he drank far more than he had intended. When he finally slept it was the sleep of drunkenness, and his dreams were violent – wild nightmares filled with the roaring of dragons and the screams and battle-oaths of mortal combat.

6

HOSTAGE!

A cock, crowing from the thatch above his head, woke Sigfrid the next morning. He yawned, sat up, then fell back again with a groan. Gods, he felt ill! The wine was taking its revenge. His insides heaved like a butter churn. He rolled over and vomited until there was nothing left in his belly, then, very gingerly, he sat up again. It was dark in the loft but a sliver of light through the manhole told him the sun must be well and truly up. An alarming thought struck him. Where was everyone? He could hear no sounds, and they had been meant to leave at dawn. Surely they hadn't gone without him?

Panic-stricken, he scrambled down the ladder. The sight that met his eyes defied comprehension. At first he thought he must be dreaming, reliving the carnage of the previous night, but this time there was one terrible difference. This time, it was not Saxon farmers who lay sprawled in death on the floor, but his own companions. They had been butchered during the night, every last one of them. Arne lay in the doorway, skewered to the ground by a knife through his throat, but most of the others had not even had time to struggle to their feet. Something, or someone, had come creeping into the hall while they slept and murdered them. And he had known nothing. He had lain snoring in the loft, not fifteen feet away, and heard only far, faint echoes of the slaughter in his dragon-haunted dreams. He clung to the ladder and shook uncontrollably.

He must have passed out, for suddenly he found himself lying on the floor and the convulsive spasms had passed. He dragged himself to his feet and tried to think. The ship! He must get back to the ship and see if she was safe. Swiftly, he crossed the room, and as he stepped outside he saw how the ground had been churned up by the hooves of horses. There had been a lot of them, too many for a band of roving outlaws or a rescue party from another farm. There was something else too. The bodies had gone. The Saxon corpses they had flung outside the previous night had vanished. Whoever had committed this outrage had taken them away, presumably for burial, and that suggested a large, confident and highly organised warband – an army almost.

And they might still be close. Fear clapped spurs to Sigfrid's sides. He fled up the hill and back towards the landing beach. As he ran he prayed to every God he could think of that the Saxons would not have found *Seasnake*. It was a forlorn hope, for in his heart he knew it must have been the smoke from the shipside campfire that had betrayed them all. When he reached the river, his worst fears were confirmed. *Seasnake* lay at the water's edge, a crumbling hulk of smoking timbers, and around her, grotesque in attitudes of death, lay the stiffening bodies of her crew. Terror crawled through Sigfrid's guts like maggots. His entire company was dead. He was alone, stranded and unprotected in a countryside swarming with his enemies. His courage abandoned him. He fell to his knees at the river's edge and began to sob like a child lost in the dark.

How long he remained like that he wasn't sure, but, gradually, his hysteria spent itself. Fear gave way to anger and a need for action. His companions had been murdered, cheated of a warrior's death. He must act quickly, or Hel would claim them for her own, dragging them down to her underworld where they would never know the glories of Valhalla. He must give them the proper rites of a hero's funeral.

It took him nearly all morning to drag the bodies back to the hall. Several times he almost collapsed with weariness, but he stuck to his task and eventually all his companions lay in a row down the centre of the hall. He had placed Arne at the centre, his head higher than the others, in tribute to his leadership. Then, dragging sheaves of straw from the loft, he spread them thickly over the bodies. At last all was ready. He lit his torch from the embers of the fire and raising it high above his head called on the Valkyries.

'Come, you choosers of the dead. These men were valiant in life and they went to their deaths as warriors. Conduct them into Odin's hall, that they may feast and fight with him until the day of Ragnarok.'

He fired the funeral pyre, then, going outside, flung the torch high on to the roof. It caught with a crackling sound. Smoke rose and small dragons of flame ran across the thatch. They danced and chuckled and swelled until their voices merged into one mighty, wind-whipped roar. The whole roof went up in flames and the building seemed to stiffen and twist like a wounded animal. As it burned, Sigfrid stood in the orange glow and screamed defiance at the sky.

Not until the flames had died and the hall had

collapsed in a ruin of blackened beams, did he abandon his vigil. Then he shook himself and looked around him as if awaking from a dream. The sun had started to dip towards the west, the wind had a bite in it that had not been there before and the sky was threatening rain. Sigfrid shivered, and remembered, too late, that he had left his warm sheepskin cloak up in the loft. He had also neglected to bring out any food, so now, not only was he alone and miles from safety, he had nothing to eat and no protection from the weather.

Despair threatened, but he fought it down. Weeping would get him nowhere. He had to think calmly. The first urgency was to get away from here, as far and as fast as possible. The smoke from his holocaust would have been visible for miles. After that he would have to work out the best route back to Thetford. It would not be easy. He could try retracing the path of the river, but that would take him into fenland, and to travel there without a boat would be impossible. The alternative, a circuitous journey across land, on foot and with no provisions, didn't bear thinking about. He remembered others who had disappeared in this country and the rumours that had spread concerning their fate.

He needed a horse, but the ones at the hall had disappeared, along with all the livestock. The East Anglian raiding party had been very thorough. Perhaps there was a house or village nearby where he could steal one. He tried to remember what landmarks they had passed the previous night. There had been something that looked like a church a couple of miles upstream – and where there was a church there must surely be houses. He would make for there.

As he turned his back on the ruined hall, rain started to fall, and it continued for the rest of the afternoon, a grim, relentless flagellation that lashed his back as he trudged along and dripped on to his head from the skeletons of trees. It soaked his clothes and turned the earth to a glue that clung to his boots and made every step an effort. It matted his hair, ran in icy trickles down his neck and sucked the warmth from his bones like a hungry leech. Its wetness drowned the embers of his courage. He kept going because there was nothing else to do, but his heart felt as numb and sodden as his body. He saw no future and no hope. In the whole world there was only misery, and the cold, eternal greyness of the rain.

Just about dusk, he found the church and, on the other side of the hill, hidden from the river, a small hamlet of perhaps a dozen houses. One dwelling stood apart from the others and probably belonged to the local thane. It was nowhere as grand as the place they had raided the previous night, but it did have its own cattle byre, and to Sigfrid that byre might have been a hall in Asgard. Where there were animals penned up for the winter there would be straw, and warmth to thaw out his frozen body. Clumsy with cold, he fumbled at the door latch and dragged it open. A pungent, animal smell wafted out to him, more beautiful to his nostrils than that of the sweetest flower or strongest ale. It was the aroma of life itself. Delirious with relief, he stumbled forward into the midst of the sleeping cattle and burrowed deeply into their bedding. His mind relinquished its hold on his exhausted body and he fell into a dreamless sleep.

When he woke, with the dawn, he ached all over. His head felt hot and heavy and he feared he was coming down with a fever. But he was alive! His clothes had dried on him during the night and his cold-crippled hands had thawed and were working again. His most urgent need now was food. It was over twenty-four hours since his last meal, and most of that he had brought up again. Memories tormented him. In Dublin, the baker would be putting the first loaves of bread into his oven just about now. Gráinne would be kindling the fire under her cauldron, and in the larger halls, thralls would be setting up spits to roast oxen for the evening's feasting. He stood up, feeling weak and dizzy, and his belly growled alarmingly.

Cautiously he opened the door and slipped out into the chill of the December morning. The cold nearly took his breath away. The sun was still no more than a reddish glow in the east, but the rain had cleared, the air was crisp and fresh and the whole world was shimmering with frost. It was going to be a beautiful day for those in a mood to appreciate it. Sigfrid was not. He shivered, and longed again for his lost cloak.

The village seemed to be still asleep. He circled it slyly, like a fox. A cock crowed somewhere among the houses and the sound put an idea into his head. Eggs! Where there was poultry there would be eggs, and though his belly lurched at the thought of sucking them raw, they would sustain him until he could find something better.

It did not take him long to find the hen house, a small beehive-shaped hut, dangerously close to one of the dwellings. With infinite caution he crept over to it and eased the door open. The hens, wakened by the beam of half-light, clucked and squawked and began to preen themselves on the perch. The cock hopped to the ground, ran out between Sigfrid's legs and flew up to the thatch where he crowed again, loudly. Sigfrid swore. He would have to move rapidly now. He could see a nest in the corner with three eggs in it. He crawled under the perch, scooped them up and backed out again as swiftly as he dared. At the doorway he stood up. It was a fraction too soon. His shoulder caught the perch and the roost exploded in a whirlwind of cackling hysteria.

Panic-stricken, Sigfrid fought his way through the screeching feather-storm. He heard the village come to life. Dogs barked, men shouted, the world reeled in a cacophony of noise and feathers. Footsteps pounded on the frozen earth, a hand grabbed his arm, a cudgel swung. White stars of pain exploded in his head and dissolved into blackness.

When Sigfrid opened his eyes again he did not know where he was. Fire burned in his head, but the rest of his body was stiff and numb with cold. What had happened to him? He seemed to be lying on the floor of a small hut and when he tried to move he realised he was trussed hand and foot, helpless as a calf in a butcher's yard. Terror gripped him. Why was he still alive? What did they want with him? He remembered the grim rumours concerning the East Anglians' treatment of prisoners and imagined what it would feel like to be flayed alive. He wished he had died at the farm with Arne and the rest.

The sun was up, but he had no idea how long he had been unconscious. Time passed slowly and painfully. Occasionally, he heard voices and sounds of activity outside, but nobody came near him. Were they simply going to leave him there to die of cold and hunger? His mind began to wander; he slept, woke, slept again, and eventually was not sure he could tell the difference.

Then he heard horses. They halted outside his prison.

There was some talking and finally the door opened. A man came in, a tall, lanky fellow with a thatch of red hair. He looked down at Sigfrid with a grin that sent shivers down the boy's spine, then without a word, reached down, twisted a hand into his hair and dragged him outside. Sigfrid gasped and screwed up his eyes against the pain. He felt himself bumped and scraped across the ground. He was hauled to his knees, held there a moment as if on display, then flung down again with a violent flourish. His mind reeled on the brink of unconsciousness. He prayed for oblivion, but the moment passed and at last, reluctantly, he forced himself to open his eyes.

He was surrounded by a large company of riders, and in their midst, looking down at him from the back of a white horse, was a figure so tall and golden he must surely be a God. Sigfrid stared at him, wondering for one insane moment if he had died and come to the gates of Asgard. A sharp kick in the ribs persuaded him otherwise and his red-headed captor said savagely, 'Well, here it is, my Lord, that Viking whelp the villagers captured for you. It doesn't look so brave now, does it? Shall I cut its throat, or shall we give it back to them to play with for a while?'

There was silence. Sigfrid gritted his teeth and prayed for a quick death. All eyes turned to the God on the white horse. Then he moved and suddenly he was only a man after all. He leaned over the neck of his horse and said in a quiet voice, 'God's death, Ulfkytel, look at him. He's only a child. I don't make war on children.'

'Child, hah! How old does a snake have to be before it is venomous?' The man called Ulfkytel scowled down at his captive. 'He is one of the animals who pillaged that farm two nights ago. Look at his clothes. I'll lay odds that is not his own blood on them.'

The big man sat for a moment without speaking. Then he swung down from his saddle and came to stand beside Ulfkytel. A shaggy wolfhound, dozing between the legs of his horse, rose and shook itself and trotted over behind him. It sniffed at the strange creature lying at its master's feet and licked Sigfrid's face with a long, wet tongue. Sigfrid squirmed and pain ran through his body. The man put a hand on the dog's collar and pulled it back. He looked down into Sigfrid's face. 'So, who are you, boy? What is your name?'

Sigfrid moved his lips, trying to find his voice. He must not let these men see his fear. 'Sigfrid Ivarsson,' he croaked, with all the arrogance he could muster. 'I am Sigfrid Ivarsson, son of the king of Dublin.'

It was a mistake. He knew it at once. A buzz of excitement ran through the group and he realised he had handed them a powerful weapon. They would make sure now that Ivar learned all about his death, in every brutal detail. He could see their eyes light up as they considered the possibilities. Only the big man seemed unmoved. He raised one golden eyebrow. 'Well, well,' he drawled. 'And tell me, Sigfrid Ivarsson, what glory seeks the son of the king of Dublin, crawling through hen roosts like a common thief?'

The men laughed, and in his humiliation Sigfrid forgot for a moment how terrified he was. He ignored the question and, scowling up at his tormentor, said insolently, 'And who are you?'

He didn't expect an answer. His body tensed instinctively against another kick or a blow, but to his astonishment the man only smiled. Leaning forward, and with that same quiet amusement in his voice, he said, 'I am Edmund Alkmundson, king of the East Anglians.'

The East Anglian king! Sigfrid knew then that he was doomed. Despite the smile and deceptive gentleness, there could be no man on earth with less reason to show him mercy than Edmund Alkmundson. Leofric's words came back to him: '*A beautiful, wrathful, golden giant. He probably eats little boys like you for breakfast.*' He shut his eyes and awaited his fate.

Above him, Ulfkytel and some of the others began a heated discussion. He could not understand all they said, but there was no mistaking their sentiments. There was a long silence, then Sigfrid felt a foot nudge him in the ribs. He opened his eyes and saw the king still looking down at him. 'You hear?' said Edmund, and there was a hardness in his voice that had not been there before. 'You hear how they call for your death? They have seen what your people did to their kinsmen. Can you give me one reason why I should spare you?'

One? He could think of a thousand. A host of petitions jostled on his tongue, but he forced them down. He was his father's son; if he had to die, he would die like a warrior. 'No,' he whispered. 'It shall not be said of Sigfrid Ivarsson, that he begged his life from a Saxon.'

'Very well.' There was another agonising silence, then, unbelievably, Edmund chuckled. 'Then it is fortunate for you, Sigfrid Ivarsson, that you are worth more to me alive than dead.'

It couldn't be! The shock of reprieve was almost painful, like a fist driven into Sigfrid's belly. He lay in the dirt and stared speechlessly at his captor. Above him another argument was developing. Ulfkytel was especially vocal. 'No, my Lord,' he pleaded, 'I know what is in your mind, but it is madness. He will never agree.'

'Then we must force him to, Ulfkytel. And this may be our only chance.'

'But he is a Viking, my lord, you cannot trust him.'

'I shall not have to, shall I, now that I have the boy.' Edmund glanced at Sigfrid again. 'Take him back to camp, Ulfkytel. Feed him and give him a bath and find him something clean to wear. He stinks like a badger after his winter sleep.'

He turned and went back to his horse. Within minutes the whole warband had departed, leaving Sigfrid alone with his keeper. Ulfkytel swore under his breath. He dragged the boy to his feet, slashed the ropes binding his wrists and ankles and held him out at arm's length, examining him with unconcealed disgust. 'Well, wolf-spawn,' he said, speaking, to Sigfrid's amazement, in the Scandinavian tongue, 'it seems I have no choice. But remember this: give me any trouble, and I'll make you wish the Lord Edmund had cut your throat himself.'

He shook the boy as a dog might shake a rat. Sigfrid swayed on his feet and tried again to speak. His comprehension was slipping, his body burned with fever, shafts of pain speared through his arms and legs. With a garbled moan, he abandoned the struggle and collapsed, unconscious into Ulfkytel's arms.

7

STALEMATE

'And I am telling you something is wrong.' Ivar scowled at his brother. 'They should have been back days ago.'

'Give them time,' said Halfdan patiently. 'Anything could have delayed them. Maybe the journey was farther than we were told. Maybe they found other, equally rich pickings along the way. Maybe ...'

'Enough! I am tired of listening to maybes. I should never have let him go.'

'And how would you have stopped him, without shaming him before all his crewmates? He is a man now. He is seventeen years old and ...'

'No, he's not. He lied to me. He has not yet turned sixteen. He is a boy, Halfdan, a rash, inexperienced boy, and it is in my heart something terrible has overtaken him. I am minded to send out a search party.'

'And lose them also? Can we risk that? Are our numbers not shrunk enough already?'

'Hel's teeth, Halfdan! It is my son we speak of.'

'And is not every man somebody's son? Warriors die, Ivar, it is in the nature of the life they lead. If Sigfrid is dead then Odin has him in his keeping; if not, then, the fates willing, he will return to you. You cannot afford this softness. We have a war to win, horses to find, a kingdom waiting for us in Northumbria.'

'You don't understand,' said Ivar bitterly. 'How could you, you who have no sons? That boy is my future, the one who will carry my name into the next generation, tell his children and his children's children of the heroism of their grandfather, even as you and I have done for Ragnar. A man's only immortality is in his sons, Halfdan. I had not realised that until now.'

Halfdan spread his hands in a gesture of hopelessness. There seemed nothing he could say.

A sentry came up. 'My Lord.'

'What is it?' growled Ivar.

'My Lord, there are messengers here, two of them,

from the East Anglian king.'

Messengers. Ivar caught his breath. Could this be news of Sigfrid or had Edmund finally decided to make peace? If so, he had picked the wrong time. Ivar was in no mood for generosity. 'Bring them here,' he commanded. 'And make sure they are disarmed and well guarded.'

The men were ushered in, surrounded by a ring of guards. Ivar scowled at them. 'So,' he sneered, 'the king of the East Anglians sends his dogs to grovel at my feet, does he?'

There was a small silence. The Saxons looked at each other. Then the taller of the two smiled. 'The king of the East Anglians sends no one where he would not go himself,' he said quietly.

Ivar stared at him. For a moment he could not believe he had heard aright. This was an audacity that bordered on madness. 'Then the king of the East Anglians is a bigger fool than I took him for,' he said finally.

'Possibly.'

'And this other man – this companion who appears to share your death wish – who is he?'

Edmund smiled again. 'This is the Lord Ulfkytel Thorkelsson, leader of my hearth troop.'

'Ulfkytel Thorkelsson?' Ivar was more confused than ever. 'That is surely no Saxon name?'

'No,' agreed the second man. 'Danish. My father was a

trader whose vessel was wrecked off this coast many years ago. He settled here and married an East Anglian.'

Ah, thought Ivar, so that is how a Saxon king learns the story of Ratatosk. 'So,' he said ominously, 'the son of a Dane in the East Anglian camp. That is indeed a thing to be remembered. But I ask again: what foolishness brings you to Thetford? Do you think to save your lives by throwing yourselves on my mercy? I offered you terms once and you rejected them.'

'You misunderstand me,' said Edmund. 'I have not come here to plead, but to reach an agreement.'

'An agreement?' Ivar looked pointedly at the ring of spears surrounding the two East Anglians, but the king only smiled.

'I have something that belongs to you,' he said, and untying a leather pouch from his belt, he pulled out a silver hammer-of-Thor pendant. He handed it silently it to Ivar. The Viking took it and felt his guts twist into a knot. It lay like a lead weight in his palm, the engraved runes winking up at him in mockery.

He closed his fist around it. 'If you have harmed him ...' he said through gritted teeth.

'Would I be here if that were so? No, your son is alive and well. And, provided we can reach agreement, he will stay that way. The decision is yours.'

The words fell like hammer blows, and with every one

of them, Ivar's anger deepened. Never before had he been backed into such a corner. Think, he urged himself, think. You are a master of strategy, use it. His mind picked its way through every option and at last he laughed. 'You are over-arrogant, Saxon,' he said softly. 'And in your arrogance you have forgotten one obvious thing. My son is in your camp. You are in mine ...' he let his hands speak the rest of the sentence.

'No,' said Edmund. 'I had not forgotten. If I am not back by nightfall my men have clear instructions.'

'Then I shall send them different ones.'

'Oh?'

'You think I cannot discover the whereabouts of your camp? All men have their breaking point, even your friend here.'

Ulfkytel made an explosive noise in the back of his throat. Edmund put a restraining hand on his shoulder. 'You do not seem to have had much success so far,' he observed cheerfully, 'and I cannot believe it has been for lack of trying. But, in any case, even if you did find my camp, it would do you little good. Sigfrid is not there. I gave orders for him to be moved, and even I do not know where they have taken him.'

Ivar decided to call his bluff. 'Then there is nothing more to discuss,' he said. 'I shall take your life and Sigfrid must take his chances. He is a Viking. He is not afraid to die.'

'Ah, yes, the pleasures of Valhalla. We Christians also believe in everlasting happiness after death, but when it beckons, few of us actually run to greet it. And there is something else I have not told you. I have instructed my priests that before your son dies, they are to baptise him into the Christian faith. Will Odin welcome into his hall one who has been dedicated to the White Christ?'

'What!' Ivar's jaw dropped. The question was an insult. What interest had Odin in the rites of the White Christ? He tried to laugh, but something cold got in the way. The sound rang hollow, even in his own ears.

'He is lying,' said Halfdan. 'His priests have no power over us.'

He was right. Logically Ivar knew it, but his fears had little to do with logic. Odin was not logical. He was capricious and he avenged insults. An unshakable image lodged itself in the Viking's mind. He pictured his son, trapped like Balder in the realm of Hel, and he knew that, whatever the cost, he could not abandon Sigfrid to such a fate.

But the alternative was to submit to this arrogant golden-haired young Saxon, the very man who, according to his plan, was to have bowed the knee to him. Ivar shuddered, and the silence stretched out to breaking point.

'What do you want from me?' he asked at last.

'Peace,' said Edmund, and he let his breath out in a

long sigh. 'We are not strong enough to drive you from East Anglia. You are not strong enough to defeat us. It is stalemate. And we both need food and shelter for the winter. Here are my terms. We will feed you while you are at Thetford and give you horses when you leave. In return, you will put an end to the killing and looting. Before you go, you will make good the damage you have done in Thetford and you will leave behind all the prisoners you now hold as thralls.'

'And Sigfrid?'

'Sigfrid will remain with me until you leave East Anglia. He will be treated with all the courtesy due to his rank, and when your ships are ready to sail, he will be returned to you.'

'And what sureties do I have for this?'

'The very best. The Lord Ulfkytel has offered to remain here as my pledge, should you so wish it.'

Fafnir's blood! A shrewd and half-Danish hostage spying on his camp for the next few months? Ivar's mind boggled at the thought. 'No,' he said hastily, 'that will not be necessary. I have prisoners already, whose lives you seem to value. They can serve as hostages.'

'As you wish. So, do we have an agreement?'

Ivar hesitated. Every ounce of his pride still urged him to refuse, to draw his sword and gut the arrogant young East Anglian where he stood. But sense prevailed. He had not survived this long on pride alone. There was a time for fighting and a time for patience. In material terms this treaty was a good one. It would secure his supplies, and he was confident that, once it was signed, Sigfrid would come to no harm in the East Anglian camp. The shame was that it was not *his* treaty. He had been out-manoeuvred and that was a humiliation he could never forget, nor forgive.

But his day would come. And when it did … He looked at his adversary, magnificent and golden in the glory of his triumph, and once more the image of Balder sprang into his mind. Beneath his cloak, his left hand curled around the hilt of his sword. *Hear me, Odin, God of battles. Here is one who is truly worthy of you. Grant me victory in Northumbria and one day I will return and give him to you.*

He nodded to Edmund. 'We have a treaty,' he conceded.

😜 😜 😜

For three days after his capture, Sigfrid lay in a fever, scarcely aware of his surroundings. Hands fed him and washed him and poured herbal concoctions down his throat. Sometimes voices hovered around him, but it was hard to tell which were real and which the product of his fever-dreams. In his delirium he returned over and over to the same nightmare. He was standing on the deck of

Seasnake – a black ship on a black and glassy sea – and the ghosts of his dead companions were all around him. White and bloody, their limbs still twisted in the stiffness of death, they accused him with staring eyes and grimly pointing fingers. 'Why did you abandon us?' they asked. 'Why did you lie asleep while we were murdered? Why are you still alive when we are dead?'

Sigfrid tried to defend himself. He argued, he pleaded, he tried to explain to them what had happened, but a rising wind plucked the words from his mouth and blew them away into the darkness. The ghosts turned from him. Like sleepwalkers, they moved to take up their places on the ship. They hauled up the sail. The helmsman set his hand to the rudder. Sigfrid was swept with terror. 'No!' he screamed. 'No, take me back to shore!' But they ignored him. Then the storm broke. Winds howled, rain fell like javelins, thunder roared and lightning whiplashed around *Seasnake's* prow. The boat shuddered, then leapt, like a hound freed from the leash, and Hel opened her gates and sucked her in. Down, down, down she plummeted, in a whirling maelstrom, deeper and deeper into everlasting blackness. Suddenly there was a jolting crash and Sigfrid found himself in bed once more, sobbing and soaked in sweat, with Saxon voices murmuring above him.

They had brought him to a fowler's hut, somewhere in

the marshes, and Ulfkytel, on his return from Thetford, had been appointed to look after him. That much he discovered as he slowly clawed his way back to strength. It was a task for which the redheaded Dane clearly had little stomach. Ulfkytel was scrupulous in carrying out his duties – making sure his patient was clothed and cleaned and properly fed, but he made it plain he was only obeying orders and that, had he been given his own way, Sigfrid would have ceased to trouble him a long time ago.

There were times when Sigfrid himself wished he were dead. As his fever receded, the nightmares became less frequent, but even when he was well enough to separate dream from reality he could not shake off the horror of his experiences. Death had never touched him before. He had seen it, dealt it out many times himself, but it had meant nothing. Men died, others took their place. It was all part of the great adventure, an enemy trodden underfoot or a friend gone to Valhalla in a cloud of glory. But there had been no glory in Arne's death. It had been sickening, obscene. He could still see those staring eyes, those contorted limbs, the body skewered to the floor. Arne had been his mentor, had guided him, protected him, taught him everything he knew. Now he was gone. Between one breath and another the life had been driven out of him and nothing would bring it back.

But he, Sigfrid, had survived. Why? What whim of the

Gods had determined that he should spend that night hidden in the loft? Had Odin protected him, or was it some spiteful prank of Loki Mischief Maker? In his more bitter moments Sigfrid suspected Loki, for surely death would have been better than his present situation. He was devastated when he learnt of the deal Edmund had made with his father. It was Ulfkytel who told him. The lanky Dane took delight in repeating, word for word, everything that had been said at Thetford, and Sigfrid cringed inwardly as he pictured the confrontation. How could his father bear the shame? What must he think of the son who had been the cause of it? The humiliation was almost too great to endure.

He wanted to hit back, to avenge himself on these men who had held him like a knife to his father's throat, but he was powerless and that knowledge only heightened his frustration. In his despair he resorted to truculence. He was insolent, spat obscenities at his captors or refused to speak to them at all, and, in between, spent hours dreaming up elaborate plans for escape. None of them ever came to anything. Ulfkytel seemed able to read his mind as easily as Ubbe had read the runes, and eventually it was Ulfkytel who convinced him he was wasting his time.

'What makes you think your father wants you back, anyway?' the Dane demanded one day after yet another bid for freedom had ended in humiliating failure.

Sigfrid stared at him. 'What do you mean? Of course he wants me back.'

His captor laughed. 'Use your brains, boy. He's got what he wants. Your only value to him now is if you stay here and behave yourself. Make no mistake, your father is the winner in this bargain. He has the food he needs, eventually he will have his horses, and he can rest secure in the knowledge that no more of his ships will disappear in the marshes. What is more, he did not have to sue for terms. He can tell everyone they were forced on him by your capture, and blame you for any shame he feels.'

'No.' Sigfrid put his face in his hands. He felt sick to the very core of his being. 'You're lying,' he said. 'You're lying!' He flung his head up. He felt his hands curl into fists. He longed to smash them into Ulfkytel's face, but at the last moment he restrained himself. He had no illusions regarding Ulfkytel. To the Dane, 'alive and well' simply meant 'not dead'. If provoked, he was quite capable of beating Sigfrid to within an inch of his life and arguing the rights and wrongs of it later. Sigfrid was powerless. Even retaliation was denied him. He dropped his hands and turned away, hoping Ulfkytel would not see the misery in his face.

The Dane laughed. 'You're learning,' he said, and he went away, leaving Sigfrid to consider his position.

8

THE FALCON BEARER

With peace secured, the East Anglian king announced that he would take his hearth troop to the royal hall at Beodricesworth to celebrate the mid-winter festival that honoured the birth of their White Christ. Sigfrid feigned indifference when Edmund came in person to bring him the good news.

'I thought you would be pleased,' said his captor, glancing around the small hut that had comprised Sig-frid's entire world for the past two weeks. 'You must be getting tired of this place.'

Sigfrid shrugged. 'I exchange one prison for another.

What difference will it make?'

'That depends on you. You are a hostage and entitled to be treated as such. Give me your word that you will not try to run away and there need be no prison. You can ride into Beodricesworth as my guest, share my table, and enjoy the hospitality of my hall.'

'And if I refuse?'

'Then you will be carried in, bound hand and foot in a baggage cart, and spend your days sitting in a corner, chained to the wall like a disobedient puppy.'

Chained like an animal? Dependent on his captors for every necessity of life? It was a fate almost too hideous to think about. But so too was the alternative. 'Do your worst,' Sigfrid spat. 'I have no word to give. It would be an insult to my honour.'

'Your honour, or your pride?' Edmund's mouth twitched in a wry smile. 'You must learn to tell the difference. There is no shame in being a hostage. All kings take pledges from their thanes. I have many young men among my own hearth companions whose fathers have placed them there in token of their loyalty. Your father has merely done the same. He agrees to our treaty, and gives you to me in surety. What is the difference?'

There was a difference, and they both knew it. Nevertheless, Sigfrid did, in the end, bow to necessity. He was a bargaining chip, an expendable playing piece in a deadly game of hnaftaefl. If he refused his word and did eventually manage to escape, what would be the result? It would only destroy the treaty, and probably Ivar's chances of getting to Northumbria. No, rightly or wrongly, he was compelled to stay.

'Very well,' he said sulkily. 'If my father wishes me to stay, so be it. I will promise. But do not think I do it willingly or because I am afraid of prison.'

'It is in my mind, Sigfrid Ivarsson,' said the king solemnly, 'that there is little in this world you fear, except the loss of dignity. But do not despair. I accept your word without demanding your friendship. You may hate me as much as you wish, if it consoles you.'

It did console him, for a while. But hatred is a wearisome companion. Besides, you couldn't truly hate a man you admired, and it was impossible not to have a sneaking admiration for Edmund Alkmundson. A man who had stood unarmed before the great Ivar Ragnarsson and bested him in a battle of wits could hardly be treated with contempt. Sigfrid knew also, although he would never have admitted it, that but for Edmund, he would probably be dead by now, in Valhalla or, more likely, since his death would have been a shameful one, a prisoner of Hel in gloomy Niflheim.

The people of Beodricesworth turned out in their hundreds to greet their king. They lined the streets, cheering and waving cloaks and banners. An offering for victory was made to the White Christ, but Sigfrid refused point-blank to enter the portals of his holy place. He was curious, though, about the beliefs of his captors. 'Where do your warriors go when they die?' he asked the king that evening at table. 'Does the White Christ have a heroes' hall for them?'

'He does.' Humbert, the East Anglian bishop, leaned forward to take over the conversation. 'All who leave this world in a state of grace are taken up to heaven.'

Taken up? Sigfrid frowned thoughtfully. Ah, so the White Christ must have Valkyries just as Odin did. He had no idea what a 'state of grace' might be, but he assumed it had something to do with bravery. 'And those not fit for heaven?'

'They go to hell.'

'Hel? Don't you mean Niflheim? Hel is the name of the giantess who rules there.'

'No,' said Humbert gently. 'Hell is the kingdom of Satan and all the fallen angels. The wicked – those who reject the teachings of Christ – are cast down there into everlasting flames. Only the virtuous may enter heaven.'

'And who are the virtuous?'

'Those who are free from sin.'

'Sin?' Sigfrid was becoming more confused by the minute.

'Murder, rape, theft – the crimes you and your pagan friends commit. Those are sins.'

'Oh.' Sigfrid was astonished. This White Christ seemed ridiculously choosy about his company. What did murder or theft have to do with the Gods? They were purely legal matters. Odin didn't care how many men you murdered or stole from, as long as you were brave and died a warrior's death. 'And what do they do in heaven, your warriors? Do they fight by day and revive to feast and drink by night?'

'Indeed, they do not.' Humbert looked scandalised.

Edmund laughed. 'The truth is, we don't know,' he admitted. 'No one has ever come back to tell us.'

'Besides,' put in Ulfkytel, 'we shall have better ways to pass the time. Unlike your warriors we shall have our womenfolk with us.' And he winked across the table at his wife.

Everyone laughed, except Humbert, and the conversation passed to other matters. Sigfrid turned the information over in his mind. Heaven, Hell, Valhalla, there were similarities as well as differences, it seemed, between his beliefs and those of his captors. He must ask one day if there was a Christian Ragnarok, the day when the world would end in bloodshed and destruction. Edmund's statement about what heaven was like intrigued him, too. *We don't know. No one has ever come back to tell us.'* But had anyone ever come back from Valhalla? A chilling thought struck him. Suppose these Christians were right? If 'virtue' was what counted, if anyone could get into Valhalla, even those who died in their beds, what value was there in a warrior's life? What had been the point of Arne's death? And Ubbe's runes – surely they didn't consistently lie to him? He didn't want to consider the possibility, so he blocked it from his mind.

🜨   🜨   🜨

The falcon circled on the frosty air, climbing steadily to reach her pitch. With effortless grace she spiralled upward, and then she 'waited on', circling the line of beaters, her eyes raking the gorse for any quarry they might flush. The men advanced slowly until at last a partridge broke from cover ahead of them and rose in a flurry of clumsy wings. The hawk spotted him. For a fraction of a second she hung motionless, then her head tipped forward, her wings curved back and she swooped, swift and deadly as a flighting arrow. Her shadow fell across the partridge. It swerved desperately, but it was too late. The hawk struck with the force of a thunderbolt. Her talons raked its back, scattering feathers like a swirl of soft, brown snow. The partridge plummeted to earth, landing with a heavy thud and the falcon glided down to settle on the still quivering body.

The watchers on the nearby hillside shouted in approval. 'A strike,' cheered Ulfkytel. 'The cleanest I've seen all day.'

Edmund grinned and raised a triumphant fist. 'Didn't I tell you she'd repay all those hours of training?' He swung from his horse and, tossing the reins to Ulfkytel, went down the hill to take up his bird. He called to her as he approached, caressing her with his voice, praising her for her speed and beauty. He touched the back of her feet and she stepped back obediently onto his glove, looking about her with calm, arrogant eyes for the reward she had come to expect after a kill. Edmund fed her a morsel of pigeon flesh and while she was eating, fastened the leash to her jesses and secured it between his fingers. Finally, he slipped the hood over her head and made his way back up the hill to his companions.

Sigfrid watched him enviously. All his life he had wanted to own a hawk, but Hoskuld had maintained they were a waste of time. Farmers have no time for idle games, he had said. And the Viking life was too nomadic for the long, patient hours needed to train a bird. If he'd stayed in Dublin, perhaps ... but he hadn't and you couldn't have everything.

Edmund handed his bird to Ulfkytel while he remounted, then took her back again. He turned to look at Sigfrid. 'Would you like to hold her?' he asked.

Sigfrid's mouth fell open. How could he possibly have known? He shrugged, trying not to show how thrilled he was.

'Hold out your hand, then. Ulfkytel, lend me a gauntlet.'

Sigfrid nudged his horse in close to Edmund's and pulled on the glove Ulfkytel tossed to him. He extended his arm and, gently, Edmund transferred the hawk onto his fist. She fidgeted for a moment then settled. Edmund smiled. 'See, she trusts you,' he said.

Sigfrid felt a thrill of pride. Before he could stop himself he heard his voice asking, 'May I fly her?'

The East Anglian thought for a moment. 'I don't see why not,' he said at last. 'She has not been overworked today, one more flight will not harm her. But rest her first, while someone else has a turn.'

Again words leapt unbidden into Sigfrid's mouth. 'Thank you,' he said.

Ulfkytel gave a snort of laughter. 'Well, now I've heard everything.'

His king silenced him with a look.

They hunted for the rest of the afternoon, taking in a wide sweep of land west of the town and all day Sigfrid carried the hawk like a badge of honour. She grew heavy on his arm, but when Edmund suggested he give her to the cadger, to carry with the other birds, he shook his head fiercely. She was still on his fist when they turned for home. Everyone was in high spirits. The sport had been good and there was a banquet to look forward to that night. It was to honour St Stephen, who was apparently a great hero in the halls of the White Christ. Sigfrid wondered briefly why Christian heroes always seemed to be men who had met a shameful death, but he didn't ask. A feast was a feast – did it really matter whom it honoured?

They were about a mile from the town, coming down through a stand of pine trees, when they heard sounds of merriment ahead, and riding out of the trees they came upon a group of men and boys tramping towards the town. They were cheering and singing and their leader carried a willow pole from which hung the small, be-ribboned body of a wren. When they saw the royal party they stopped and Ulfkytel rode forward, pretending to challenge them. 'What wolfshead company is this,' he demanded, laughingly, 'that disturbs the king's peace in so riotous a fashion?'

The man with the willow pole pushed his way forward. 'No outlaws, my Lord, but Odi blacksmith and some of his fellow tradesmen.' He made a low bow to Edmund. 'God's greeting, my Lord the King, we mean you no disrespect, but today, by tradition we have been seeking a king of a different kind, and see, we have found him.'

He raised aloft his trophy and the ribbons adorning the

tiny corpse fluttered bravely in the wind. Sigfrid, watching, thought suddenly of Dublin. The Irish, he remembered, had hunted wrens at this same time last year. It seemed a strange sport to him, but then many things the Irish and East Anglians did were strange.

The men were clearly expecting some gift for their wren-king. Edmund unfastened his silver cloak pin and tossed it down to them. 'Good health and joy to your king, my friends,' he told them. 'And good luck to your celebrations.'

The blacksmith caught the gift in a huge fist and held it up for everyone to see. His companions cheered and whistled and thumped staves on the ground in a gesture of approval. Edmund laughed. Ulfkytel tossed down a few coins from the pouch he carried at his belt and the rest of the party also offered gifts. The townsmen voiced their thanks and continued on their way, exclaiming noisily over their unexpected good fortune.

Sigfrid stared after them. To him the encounter had seemed an absurd piece of pageantry 'Why the wren?' he wondered aloud. 'A hawk or even a raven I could understand, but why, in the name of all the Gods, a wren?' He shook his head. To his mind there had been something almost pathetic about that forlorn little bundle of feathers.

Edmund chuckled. 'For myself,' he told Sigfrid, 'I am

thankful it is a wren. In an age gone by, it would have been me hanging from that pole. The wren is the "summer king", the "corn king" who must die each winter for his people. His blood will renew and fertilise the earth and in the spring he will rise again with the new crops.'

'Hah! Let you make sure such heresy does not come to Humbert's ears,' warned Ulfkytel, with a laugh. 'He would berate you soundly for encouraging such pagan rites.'

'We have no custom like this in Denmark,' said Sigfrid, though he thought briefly of Balder and how everything in the realms of both men and Gods had shed tears in an attempt to raise him from the dead.

'It is a very ancient ritual,' said the king. 'And it did not start, I think, with our people. It came down to us from another race, the men who held this land before us.' He looked up at the sky. 'And now we must make a move. There is snow in those clouds, if I am not mistaken, and I have no wish to get caught in a blizzard.'

He nudged his horse forward and the rest of the troupe followed him. Sigfrid hesitated for a moment, the memory of the dead wren still uncomfortable on his mind. Then he shrugged and, setting his heels to his own mount, rode off after the others, the falcon standing proud and silent on his wrist.

9

NOT SO DIFFERENT

It was odd, thought Sigfrid, how one's enemies could turn out to be people so much like oneself. The East Anglians looked like Scandinavians. Indeed, Edmund's tall, broad-shouldered frame and corn-gold hair made him the very embodiment of a Viking hero. Their language was similar, they laughed at the same jokes and they shared the same zest for feasting and consuming large quantities of ale and mead.

There were differences though, and they were subtle ones, which made them all the more disconcerting. He glanced around the hall – they were staying at Hellesdon now, in a new building erected over the ashes of the one Ivar had burned six months earlier. Despite its grandeur, it reminded Sigfrid more of Hoskuld's farm than Ivar's mead hall in Dublin. Dublin was a warrior society, purely masculine. Few of Ivar's men had wives – not real ones, anyway, you couldn't count Irish slave women – and those who were married seldom brought their wives into the hall. Here, women regularly shared the benches with their menfolk and though the men might boast in their cups of their prowess with the sword, talk turned more readily to crops and stock breeding than to war.

This evening's banquet was a case in point. Far from celebrating some successful feat of arms, it was in honour of something the East Anglians called the 'christening' of Ulfkytel's baby son. The religious ceremony had taken place that afternoon and Sigfrid had been persuaded to attend. The ritual had surprised him.

'Why, it is exactly like our naming ceremony,' he told Bishop Humbert afterwards. 'In Denmark, when a new child is welcomed into the community, water is poured on him and he is marked with the sign of Thor's hammer. Then he is sat on the knee of the man who will be his patron, and that man takes a solemn oath to guide and protect him in his father's absence, just as my Lord Edmund did for Ulfkytel's son.'

Humbert's eyebrows shot up in horror. 'That is a

blasphemy,' he told Sigfrid firmly. 'You must never compare the rites of Holy Church with pagan practices. Your Gods are false. They are the instruments of Satan. There is only one true God and he will not be mocked. He punishes all those who worship idols.'

Sigfrid opened his mouth to argue, but Ulfkytel jabbed an elbow into his ribs and he changed his mind. He knew better than to provoke Ulfkytel. Instead, he waited his chance and tackled Edmund. 'I don't understand.' he said. 'Your White Christ? Bishop Humbert says he is your only God, but he told me once Christ was the *son* of God. How can he be both?'

'It is what we call a mystery,' explained the king. 'There are three persons in one God: the Father, the Son and the Holy Ghost. We call it the Holy Trinity.'

'Ah.' Light dawned. Sigfrid pictured a fierce three-headed giant. 'And did he kill off all his rivals?' he asked. 'Is that why he is the only God?'

'No,' said Edmund, 'there has only ever been one.' The corners of his mouth twitched and though he didn't quite smile, Sigfrid could tell the question had amused him. He couldn't see why; it seemed to him a perfectly logical assumption, but then Christianity didn't seem to have much to do with logic. 'Well, he must get very lonely,' he said, 'ruling up there all alone in your Christian heaven. No wonder he is so stern and jealous.'

The celebration progressed noisily. The new father, looking as proud as a warrior who has just slaughtered ten men in his first battle, carried his son around the hall for everyone to admire, while his wife, Wulfthryth, sat in the place of honour on Edmund's right, accepting their gifts and their congratulations. Sigfrid felt awkward. He had no gift to offer. He had thought of giving the infant his hammer-of-Thor amulet – it did not have the same significance for him now as when it was was his only connection with his father – but, after his conversation with Humbert, he suspected it might not be appreciated. He sat in silence, listening to the music and riddle-telling and felt for the first time a small twinge of homesickness.

It would be spring in Dublin now, just as it was in East Anglia. The snow would be melting on the southern mountains, the ice would have gone from the *Dubh Linn*. Boats would be departing, new ones arriving and along the shores the boatbuilders would be busy at their trades. Carpenters, sail-makers, plank-cutters, in workshops all up and down the muddy streets, men would be labouring at fever pitch to equip a new generation of dragon-ships.

The market would be busy too. Spring always brought a rush of merchants, eager for the spoils of last year's raiding. They would sail into the *Dubh Linn* with boats full of exotic goods: furs, glassware, fine wines and trinkets from the east, and depart with gold and slaves and jewelled ornaments plundered from the monasteries.

And Guthrum, he would be busy now, crafting dragon-heads for the new ships. Sigfrid recalled the day he had stood with Arne and watched the wood-carver at work – the patient, confident hands, the strange stylised figures emerging from the wood. If he shut his eyes he could almost reach out and touch the scene. Yet it had been a lifetime ago. There were no 'gripping beasts' in East Anglia, only effigies of the White Christ on his cross.

Someone with a loud and gravelly voice had taken the harp and was unwilling to relinquish it. The song was unfamiliar to Sigfrid and the flat tones grated on his ears, jarring him back to reality, reminding him where he was and why. Suddenly he felt the urge to be on his own. He slipped out of the hall and walked down to the river. Nobody followed him and he didn't expect them to. They knew he understood the futility of escape.

The Wensum was in full flow, swollen with the last of the melted snows, and it tumbled past its banks, foaming and gurgling in a suicidal dash towards the coast. Sigfrid sat with his back against an alder and watched it. He tossed a twig into the current and followed it with his eyes until it was swept around a bend and out of sight. I am like that twig, he thought suddenly, and the idea pleased him. These East Anglians, they are only farmers. They tread the seasons like oxen threshing corn, ploughing, sowing and harvesting in an endless circle. But I am a dragon-ship. I have launched myself on the flood tide and have no control over where it takes me.

He tossed another stick and as he watched its turbulent progress, he pictured himself and his father's whole warband as a fleet of ships, swept along on the crest of a mighty river. There was adventure waiting for them around every bend, and plunder for the taking. But there was danger too: shipwrecks, death. He recalled Arne, cast up on the shores of an East Anglian farmhouse with a dagger through his throat. And the river was unstoppable. You could not row against its tide. It swept you past rocks and fords and cataracts, always in the same direction, until finally it met the coast and spat you out into the sea.

And then what? What really happened at that journey's end? He shivered. No! He must not lose faith. He must not allow himself to doubt. If his river did cast him out onto the sea, why, then, the Valkyries would come for him and carry him away to Odin in Valhalla.

'A penny for your thoughts, Sigfrid Ivarsson.'

The voice startled him – a clear, childish voice. He turned to look at the intruder. A boy was standing at the top of the bank, a skinny, brown-haired lad who looked a couple of years younger than himself. Sigfrid had seen him occasionally about the hall and knew him to be a relative of Ulfkytel's. He scowled. 'You are easily parted from your money, lad, if you would pay a penny for what is in here.' He tapped the side of his head.

The boy shrugged and slid down the bank to sit beside him. 'What are you doing?' he asked.

'Thinking,' said Sigfrid rudely.

'Oh, I thought you might be hiding, like me, from Wulfhere and Judith.'

'From whom?' Sigfrid was bemused. 'Who are Wulfhere and Judith, and why would I want to hide from them?'

The boy laughed. 'Judith isn't a *who*, it's a *what* – a very long song. And Wulfhere is the man trying to sing it.'

'Ah, yes. I heard him,' Sigfrid chuckled. 'Why didn't someone stop him?'

'Who knows? Most of them are probably too drunk to care by now, and the sober ones are too polite. He grinned. 'But I *like* music. I couldn't bear it any longer, so I escaped and came down here to listen to the river.'

'It certainly has a better voice than Wulfhere's.' Sigfrid looked sideways at his young companion. 'What is your name, lad?'

'Leofstan,' said the boy proudly. 'Leofstan Edwaldson, sister son to the Lord Ulfkytel.'

'You have my sympathy, then, but we cannot choose our uncles. And tell me, Leofstan Edwaldson, how did you know my name?'

'Everyone knows your name. You are Sigfrid Ivarsson, son of the fierce and bloody sea-wolf, Ivar Ragnarsson.'

The fierce and bloody sea-wolf. Sigfrid smiled inwardly. The words had a daunting ring to them. 'And are you not afraid, then, to keep company with the son of so ferocious a man?'

'Afraid?' Leofstan tossed his head. 'Hah, do you take me for a coward? I am not afraid of anything. Already I am training to be a warrior and as soon as I am fifteen I am to be armour-bearer to my Lord the king.'

'Are you indeed? And when will that great day arrive?'

'Soon.'

'How soon? How old are you now?'

The youngster hesitated. 'Twelve,' he confessed sheepishly.

Sigfrid tried not to smile. 'So young and yet so brave. The Lord Edmund is indeed a lucky man.'

They sat in silence for a while. Then Leofstan said, 'They tell me you came from Dublin. Where is that?'

'In another kingdom,' said Sigfrid. 'In a country far across the sea.'

'And is that where you were born?'

'No.' To his surprise, Sigfrid found himself telling the boy about his life in Denmark, about the farm, Hoskuld, his mother, the night of the spring feast and the theft that had brought him west-over-seas to seek his father.

Leofstan listened in awe. 'I should like to cross the sea in a ship,' he said. 'Were you sea-sick?'

'Of course not!' Sigfrid pretended indignation, but then he remembered how Leofstan's boasting had amused him. 'Well, perhaps just a little,' he confessed. 'But it didn't last long.'

Leofstan laughed. 'At least you are honest. I like people who tell the truth.' He thought for a moment. 'I have a stepfather too.'

'Have you so? And does he beat you?'

'Only when I deserve it. Did you really steal Hoskuld's sword?'

'Yes.'

'Why?'

'Because he was a coward and did not deserve it.'

'Oh.' The boy thought for a moment. 'You must have wanted it very badly.'

Sigfrid didn't answer.

'What did he do that was cowardly?'

'He did nothing. That was his shame. A man does not win honour sitting on a farm and dealing out cattle to his hearth companions. A hero gives gold and arm-rings, treasures he has won with his sword from those not worthy to possess them.'

'I see. And are we unworthy? Are the Lord Ulfkytel and the Lord Edmund cowards?'

'No,' admitted Sigfrid. 'No, your uncle is no coward, and the courage of the Lord Edmund is beyond dispute, but …'

'But you still want to kill us and steal our gold and cattle?'

'Yes. No … I mean …' Sigfrid found himself at a loss to explain. He had an uncomfortable feeling he was losing this argument. How did you define heroism? He could see, dimly, the concept he wanted to defend, but words eluded him. 'You wouldn't understand,' he said, finally. 'You are only a child.'

'Hah!' Leofstan's expression told exactly what he thought of that excuse. 'I don't think you want me to understand,' he said angrily. 'Besides, I shall not be a child much longer, and you can tell your father that. Next time he attacks East Anglia he will have me to deal with as well.'

He jumped to his feet and ran back up the bank. By the time Sigfrid had followed him, he had disappeared into the lengthening shadows. Sigfrid made his way slowly back to the hall. Unwelcome thoughts nibbled at his mind. Why had the boy doubted him? Of course Hoskuld had deserved to lose his sword. Of course he had been a coward and a bully. He tried to rekindle his sense of grievance but it was difficult. Leofstan's unresentful honesty – *'Only when I deserve it'* – had stuck in his mind and refused to be dislodged.

He scowled. Hel's teeth, what was wrong with him? He must be going soft. He was a Viking. What use had he for the prattlings of a Saxon brat? And it was all Hoskuld's fault, anyway. If he was not a coward, why had he allowed himself to be robbed in his sleep? Why hadn't he woken up and fought for his sword?

He did not see Leofstan again. A few days after their meeting, Edmund moved his court south to Rendlesham and there Sigfrid remained for the rest of the spring and summer. As the months passed, he grew more and more restless. He was not ill-used. Edmund continued to treat him as a guest and even Ulfkytel mellowed sufficiently to speak to him now and then without hostility. But he was bored. Life at the East Anglian court was ordered and predictable. The fyrd had been disbanded and the king seemed to spend much of his time in council with his Witan, or dispensing justice in the various folk-moots. There were banquets and festivals, and sometimes Edmund or Ulfkytel took him hunting, but the hawks were in moult and could not be flown and anyway, hunting, whether for birds or animals, was a poor substitute for the life or death excitement of the Viking life.

He began to wonder if he would ever see real action again and in his lowest moments he grieved for *TruthSeeker*. Where was his precious sword? Hanging, no doubt, in some East Anglian mead hall, a prisoner like himself. He had failed *TruthSeeker*. He had made promises to it, promises that he could not keep. He had invested it with his honour, and now, like his honour, it was gone.

By the time the harvest had been gathered, Sigfrid had been a hostage for nine months, and his patience and behaviour were collapsing fast. In his boredom he had reverted to the ill manners of his first weeks of captivity and he suspected that, when he did leave, everyone would be thankful to see the back of him.

At last Edmund brought him the good news. 'Your father's ships have sailed under the command of your uncle Halfdan,' he told Sigfrid. 'Ivar has his horses and is preparing to depart overland with the rest of his army. Ulfkytel and I will take you to Thetford tomorrow to join him.'

Sigfrid's heart leapt, but his joy was followed almost at once by a sense of deflation. This wasn't how it was supposed to end. He should be riding back in triumph, with gold to lay before his father, and the head of at least one of his enemies, not like this, defeated and weaponless. He lay awake most of that night, debating whether to make a final bid for freedom. Even at this late hour it would surely redeem some vestige of his pride. But common sense eventually got the better of him. The treaty was still in force. If he escaped, Edmund might consider it broken. He might recall his fyrd – and Ivar had only half an army.

They left the next morning with a small escort and slept that night in the guest house of the abbey at Eye. By midday the following day, Sigfrid found himself on the banks of the Little Ouse, looking out across a flat expanse of heathland towards Thetford. It was a desolate landscape, a landscape such as Hermod must have crossed when he rode down to Niflheim to plead for the return of Balder. Nevertheless it afforded good protection for the town. No one could approach it without being seen.

Edmund halted just under half a mile from the town. He beckoned Sigfrid to ride up beside him. 'So.' he said. 'Here we part company. I am not fool enough to walk into the bear's cave a second time.'

Sigfrid looked towards his father's stronghold. Beyond the walls he could see the smoke rising from hundreds of hearths. The great wooden gates had been dragged open and he could see men in the entrance. He felt his pulse quicken. It had really happened. He was free, so abruptly, so undramatically. All he had to do was ride down there and ... he scowled at Edmund. 'How can I trust you?' he asked. 'How do I know you haven't ordered one of your men to put an arrow in my back?'

Edmund smiled. 'Because I am neither an oath-breaker

135

nor a fool. How many men does your father have? How many have I brought? Is it not I who must trust him – that he will not pursue us when we leave.'

'Oh.' Sigfrid hadn't thought of that.

The king smiled again. 'But I do trust him, in this if in nothing else. He has kept his word and you have kept yours, and it cannot always have been easy for you. Before you go, I would like to give you something.' He turned in the saddle. 'Ulfkytel?'

The red-headed thane rode up with a bundle in his arms. It was a sheepskin cloak, white and thick, almost identical to the one Sigfrid had lost in the fire, and it had been rolled into a long tube as if to conceal an arrow or a spear-shaft. He handed it to Edmund. 'I hope you know what you are doing, my Lord,' he said gruffly.

'I do,' said Edmund. He unwrapped the bundle and, with a catch in his heart, Sigfrid saw *TruthSeeker*. He stared at it, utterly lost for words, and at last in his confusion resorted to defensiveness. 'What generosity is this?' he jeered. 'You know full well where we are bound, yet you put a sword in my hands and send me out to kill your fellow Christians.'

Edmund smiled. 'You have behaved with courage and dignity in East Anglia, Sigfrid Ivarsson, and I respect you for it. You have earned your sword. As for Northumbria, her kings have both been warned. If they would rather fight each other than defend their kingdom, they must bear the consequences.' He looked at the sword. 'It is a fine weapon. What do you call it?'

'*TruthSeeker*,' said Sigfrid.

'*TruthSeeker*. A strange name for a weapon of destruction.' The king smiled again and put both cloak and sword into Sigfrid's hands. 'Well, Sigfrid Ivarsson, I hope you find the truth you are looking for. And I hope when you do find it that you recognise it. Do we part as friends?'

Sigfrid hesitated. It was nearly impossible not to respect this man, and his last act of generosity almost demanded friendship. But as he strapped *TruthSeeker* to his hip, he remembered again how he had come to lose it. He saw the blood on the floor of the hall and Arne's terrible, staring eyes. 'No,' he said. 'The blood of my companions stands between us. If we meet again, it will be my duty to avenge them.'

He nudged his horse forward and rode down towards the town, proud and tall in the saddle, his back as rigid as a spear-shaft. At the gates, when he felt sure the East Anglians would no longer be looking, he turned to glance back the way he had come – and saw, to his chagrin, that Edmund was still watching him.

10

TO ARMS! TO ARMS!

The gates of Thetford closed behind him, the walls embraced him like a coat of mail. He was safe again, back amongst his own.

But he had still to face his father.

Ivar greeted him in the moot-hall. 'So.' he said, wearing his granite mask. 'He has sent you back to us, then.'

'Yes,' said Sigfrid.

'And you are well? He did not ill-use you?'

'No.'

'Hmm. Then it would seem the king of the East Anglians is at least a man of his word.'

'Yes.'

Father and son looked at one another and the silence stretched uncomfortably. Sigfrid was floundering. What was expected of him. An apology? An explanation?

'I … I'm sorry …' he faltered.

'For what?'

'I shamed you.'

Ivar shrugged. 'You were captured. I agreed to terms. No shame; it happens in war.'

'Yes, but …' He thought of the other thing. 'Arne,' he said. 'He's dead. They're all dead.' To his horror, Sigfrid felt his eyes fill with tears and before he could stop himself he was blurting out the whole sickening story.

Ivar listened impassively.

'Arne knew the dangers,' he said when Sigfrid finally stopped. 'He accepted them, as we all do. You gave him a warrior's funeral. It was enough. He is in Valhalla and crying will not bring him back.'

'I will avenge him,' swore Sigfrid, and his hand dropped to touch the hilt of *TruthSeeker*.

Ivar smiled. 'We both will,' he promised. 'I too have unfinished business with Edmund of East Anglia.'

And that, it seemed, was to be the end of the matter. Ivar never spoke of it again and Sigfrid did not see any reason to remind him. He would always recall his months of captivity with anger and embarrassment, but as he slipped back into his old life, he was astonished at how quickly the memory became more like a bad dream than something that had really happened.

There was little time, anyway, for dwelling on the past. Ivar's warriors, restless and war-hungry after their winter lay-up, were eager to be on the move again and Ivar himself was anxious to rejoin his ships. Within days, Sigfrid found himself back in the saddle, bound for Northumbria. Edmund had not cheated them over the promised horses. They were strong, healthy animals, and big – much bigger than the sturdy little Irish ponies Sigfrid was used to. As he rode northward through Mercia, with his sword at his side and the new cloak pinned around his shoulders, he felt like Sigurd the Volsung astride his incomparable Grani.

The journey passed uneventfully. If Burgred, the king of Mercia, was aware of their presence in his kingdom he clearly felt it wiser to pretend otherwise, and thanks to the supplies provided under the terms of their treaty with the East Anglians, the Vikings had little need for raiding or looting along the way. They pressed on steadily and soon the day came when Sigfrid, riding in the front ranks of the company, came over the crest of a hill and saw in the distance the river Humber stretching out before him. He drew rein and gazed at it. It reminded him of a snake, a great serpent, powerful and unstoppable, winding its way eastward to the sea. It was their road into Northumbria, the gull's path that would lead them to victory. The rest of the company came crowding on to the hilltop around him. A cheer ran through the ranks, and as Ivar led them down on to the plain even the horses instinctively quickened their pace, seeming to know their journey was nearly over.

Less than an hour later they found Halfdan and the ships. He had beached them in a sheltered bay on the southern shore of the estuary and set up a camp to welcome the saddle-weary riders. Tents and awnings had been erected, meat was cooking, whole bullocks turning on spits above beds of burning logs. Pennants hung from every tent pole and fluttered from the masts of all the ships, while high above them, arrogant in its majesty, the Lodbrok raven stretched its pinions on the wind. Sigfrid caught his breath. The place looked more like a market than a war camp. Halfdan must feel very sure of himself, to flaunt his presence so openly in such an undefended spot.

Ubbe had joined his brother in his camp and they both greeted the new arrivals with boisterous enthusiasm. But, once the first pleasantries had been dispensed with, Ivar came straight to the business in hand. 'So,' he said, casting a long, critical look around the camp, 'you are set up in some style here. It would seem my plans have already started to bear fruit?'

His brothers grinned at each other. 'Like apple trees in autumn,' affirmed Halfdan. 'Ubbe has played his part well.'

Ubbe chuckled. 'It was easy. It fell out just as you predicted. I made a great show of carrying my sword to the ex-king Osbert and aided him in a few skirmishes against Aelle, the man he claims has stolen his throne. Now the fool is convinced of my loyalty and even believes I have summoned you here to swell his ranks.'

They all laughed. 'He is in for a shock, then,' promised Ivar, 'for it is in my mind that Odin is truly guiding us. And I have not forgotten my promise – a king of men on the wings of the king of birds.' His voice took on a faraway quality and his eyes gazed out across the water as if, in his mind, he too were taking flight.

'And which of them will you choose?' asked Halfdan.

'What?'

'Which of the kings do you mean to sacrifice to the all-Father?'

There was a silence. Ivar seemed to be having trouble disengaging from his vision. Then, finally he shook himself and came back to earth again. He roared with laughter. 'Why, both of them,' he declared, 'if my luck is good enough.' He slapped his brother on the back. 'A double offering! The skalds will sing from now till Ragnarok of how the son of Lodbrok hallowed his victories.'

Both kings! Sigfrid felt a thrill run through his body. *'When you give a man to Odin at the point of your sword ...'* Was this his opportunity? If there were two sacrifices, might his father allow him ...?

But Ivar had already moved on to other things. 'So tell me, Ubbe,' he said. 'You have been our ears and eyes in this place for over a year now. How lies the country? Where should we strike first?'

'All in good time,' said Ubbe. 'First, we have food and drink prepared for you. You must eat and have something to wash the dust from your throat. We can talk over our cups.'

He put an arm around his brother's shoulder and the three of them moved off towards one of the tents. Sigfrid hesitated, uncertain whether he was supposed to follow. Ivar turned and grinned at him. 'You too, boy. You must be hungry and thirsty, and it will do you good to sit in on our council. But let you remember, you are here to listen and learn, not to offer an opinion.'

Sigfrid nodded.

'Now,' said Ubbe, setting down his empty drinking horn. 'I'll show you what I propose.' He squatted on the floor and with a stick began to trace lines in the dirt. 'This is the town of York. It sits, so, in the crook of an elbow of land, where the river Foss flows into the Ouse. It is the chief town of Northumbria and easy to defend. That is where you should make your base. Take York and you will control Northumbria from the river Humber to the mountains.'

Ivar frowned and pulled at his beard. 'But if it is so easy to defend, will it not also be difficult to capture?'

His brother grinned. 'I said "easy to defend", not "well defended". Osbert, as I told you, believes we are in his pay, and Aelle is away in the north, trying to rally support for his own cause. York is as innocent of defenders as a nunnery.'

'And in ten days' time,' said Ivar thoughtfully, 'it will be All Saints' Day.'

'All Saints Day?' Sigfrid didn't see the significance. The question popped out before he remembered his orders, but his father didn't seem to mind.

'It is a festival,' he explained, 'one of the great feast days celebrated by the Christians.' He chuckled. 'We learnt to make good use of them in Ireland. There will be markets and banquets and religious ceremonies. The town will be crowded with visitors and no one will be prepared for an attack.'

'We shall descend on them like foxes on a hen-roost,' boasted Halfdan, 'and they will behave exactly like frightened hens, squawking and screeching and doing nothing but getting under each other's feet.'

'And it is a rich town,' added Ubbe. 'There will be plunder enough for everyone. And captives to trade as thralls. We'll have more than we know what to do with.'

'We'll have a kingdom too,' said Ivar softly. 'The one you spoke of in Dublin, Halfdan. The one we will not have to share with Olaf.'

'Exactly,' said Halfdan.

They all turned to look at Sigfrid.

Sigfrid scowled. He was still smarting from Ubbe's unfortunate reference to chicken-roosts. 'If Olaf is still alive,' he muttered. 'We have had no news from him.'

His father grinned. 'Oh but we have,' he said. 'He sent a messenger to Thetford not long before you returned. And he is very much alive. It is Audgils who is dead.'

'Audgils, dead?' Sigfrid remembered again that terri-fying night in Dublin, and felt a glow of satisfaction. 'Was it at Olaf's hand?'

'How else? And in a fight over a woman, so I am told.'

'That would be likely.' Sigfrid thought of his father's reference to a kingdom in Northumbria. 'Do you really have it in your mind to make a permanent settlement here?'

'Perhaps. Many of my crews are growing land-hungry. They have been campaigning with me for years – first in Ireland and now over here. Their bodies are ageing, their sword arms grow heavy and their thoughts turn to farms and families. Even a berserker cannot fight forever.'

Sigfrid tried to imagine growing old. A vision flitted through his mind of a lush, green-pastured hillside in Ireland, a hall similar to Hoskuld's, and himself sitting in the high seat with a woman at his side. He pushed it away. What did he want with farms and marriage? Hadn't Sigurd the Volsung's troubles all started on the day he took a wife? 'My sword arm is not heavy,' he declared.

'Not yet, perhaps.' His father laughed. 'But in time even you will grow tired. And would you not like to be King of York?'

'No,' said Sigfrid. 'I would rather be Sigfrid *TruthSeeker*.'

'Sigfrid *TruthSeeker*. Sword and man alike, eh? And tell me, Sigfrid *TruthSeeker*, what is it, this truth that you are seeking?'

Sigfrid felt rather than heard the laughter in his father's voice. 'How should I know?' he said haughtily. 'If I had it I would not have to seek it, would I? Besides, it was you who gave me the name at our first meeting.'

'Did I?' said Ivar, and then, after a moment's thought, 'So I did, I had forgotten.' And he turned his attention back to the map on the floor.

The pre-dawn air had an icy bite to it. Sigfrid shivered and huddled deeper into his cloak. He was standing on the bank of the Foss with the rest of the war band and, like everyone else, gazing up in awe at the massive wall that blocked their way. So this was the palisade of York. It looked as formidable as one of the walls of Asgard. How in the name of Loki were they ever going to breach it?

He hoped Ubbe knew what he was doing. His uncle had laughed when Ivar had asked the same question that first day in camp. 'Trust me,' Ubbe had said. 'They may look strong, but they are very old, built by a people who ruled here long before the Saxons. Mortar has crumbled, stones and bricks have collapsed, and the Northumbrian kings have been too busy quarrelling with each other to repair the damage. A tap or two in the right place and you will have a hole big enough to drive a herd of cattle through.'

'And you know this "right place"?' Ivar had asked. 'You can lead us to it?'

'Like a bird flying to its nest.' Ubbe had laughed again and tapped a finger against the side of his nose.

Well, he had better be right, or they would be trapped here in full view, like flies against a spider's web, when the sun came up. He watched as his uncle chose a team of men and set them to work on a section of the wall, a section where Sigfrid could now see long zig-zag cracks running down the stonework. The men worked quietly and unhurriedly, chipping at the mortar with their spears and removing the bricks and stones one by one.

Why don't they go faster? worried Sigfrid. It will be dawn soon, and that wall looks as thick as a mountainside. But Ubbe knew what he was doing. The far side of the wall had collapsed years before, leaving only a thin veneer of stonework. Suddenly, with a clinking and a clattering, a wide section tumbled inwards, revealing a hole as big as the side of a house. Sigfrid had to restrain himself from cheering. His heart began to thump and his mind flew back to a night twelve months before, when he had stood on a hillside in East Anglia and looked down with Arne on a sleeping farm. *TruthSeeker* seemed to quiver at his side as if hungry for blood and action.

'Intruders! To arms! To arms! Intruders!' A voice shattered the silence. A horn blast ripped the night apart. A hail of stones clattered down from the top of the wall. Sigfrid ducked. Someone screamed. The man beside him dropped like an arrow-shot deer. The whole company flung itself at the wall, pushing, kicking, wrenching and tearing with their hands. Another, larger section collapsed and suddenly they were through, streaming into the town like water through a ruptured dam.

Sigfrid was swept forward on the tide. Around him was chaos. Men were coming from everywhere, pouring from buildings like rats from a burning barn, shouting, roaring, waving shields and weapons. The world was a maelstrom of struggling bodies and in the darkness it was hard to distinguish friend from foe. A face half covered with a beard loomed up in front of him. He lunged at a point beneath it. *'Crowd him. Keep your shield up. Don't let him come in over the top of you.'* Arne's lessons echoed in his head. He thrust again, felt his blade sink home and then pulled it out, drenched in blood. The face disappeared.

Another took its place. *'Thrust, retrieve, thrust, keep moving. Mind your back, watch his sword arm. Don't stand too long in one position.'* He caught sight of his father, solid as a rock in the midst of the mayhem, laying about him with a huge two-handed battle axe. He began to fight his way towards Ivar. A sword slashed at his shoulder, he raised his shield to deflect it, thrust upward with his own blade. The sword-wielder grunted and slumped to the ground in front of him.

He tripped over the body, fell, scrambled up, struggled forward again. A spear raked his helmet, jarring and half stunning him. He went down, rolling instinctively as the weapon jabbed towards him. Fire flashed through his side. The spear stuck quivering in the ground beside him. Its owner retrieved it and raised it to strike again. Sigfrid groped for his shield. The Saxon grinned, his hand tightened on the spear, then inexplicably he stiffened, coughed, and toppled forward on top of Sigfrid, spilling blood all over him.

Sigfrid struggled out from under the corpse and tried

to stand. His head reeled, his eyes refused to focus, his ripped flank burned as if someone had rubbed salt in it. He stumbled, staggered a couple of paces and collapsed again. Hands, whether friendly or hostile he could not tell, lifted him and carried him clear of the fighting.

Voices were floating above him and someone dabbed with a wet cloth at his injured side. He swore and flung out a hand to ward it off.

'Lie still,' said one of the voices. 'You will start it bleeding again.'

His father! Sigfrid opened his eyes. He was lying on a pallet in a long, high-roofed hall. The room was quiet; wintery sunlight streamed in through the doorway and the faces around him were friendly ones. He moved his head cautiously. One of Ivar's men was cleaning his wounds and the Viking leader himself was looking down on him with anxious eyes. Sigfrid tried to recall the events that had brought him here. 'I fell,' he remembered at last. 'Where am I? Did we win?'

'We won,' Ivar patted his shoulder reassuringly. 'We won well. You fought like a hero. You were wounded, but it is not serious and you are safe now in the moot-hall. How do you feel?'

'Sore,' said Sigfrid. 'And tired.' He tried to sit up, but immediately the pain from his wound shot through his body like an arrow throust. The room began to whirl around him and he fell back on his pallet. Alive, he thought triumphantly. Alive and safe and the battle fought and won. *'You fought like a hero,'* his father had said. He allowed himself to slide back into sleep.

11

THE SHADOW OF A RAVEN

Sigfrid stood with his father on the city wall and looked down over the Vale of York. Nearly five months had passed since the day they had forced their way into the town. His wound had healed, though he would carry the scar of it as a badge of honour all his life. Winter had given way to spring. The last snows had melted on the ploughlands and now a fierce March wind was drying out the ground. Shoots of barley were already pushing up through the rich soil. Sigfrid noted them with surprise. He recalled the long winters in Denmark and the meagre coastal soil that had comprised most of

Hoskuld's holding. 'This is good country,' he said approvingly. 'A farmer would not have to struggle here.'

Ivar smiled. 'An eye for land, eh? Your stepfather must have taught you something, after all.'

Sigfrid stiffened. 'He ground my nose into it. I ploughed and sowed seed for him and spread dung like a thrall. And even a thrall knows good ploughland when he sees it.'

The angry words rose automatically to his lips, but even as he spat them out, other memories intruded. Hoskuld harvesting, soaked in sweat and working twice as fast as anyone else. *'Put some guts into it, boy. On this farm, everyone works. You don't coax crops out of the ground by sitting on your backside giving orders.'* Hoskuld at midnight, up to his elbows in blood and ooze, dragging a foal from the body of its labour-spent dam. *'Of course you are tired, boy. Of course it stinks, but you have to learn. This will be your farm one day, and your horse. You can't trust thralls with a job like this. They don't care enough.'*

How his stepfather had driven him, and how he had hated the man. But in his resentment, he had failed to realise one thing – the tyrant who worked others so remorselessly never asked them to do what he would not do himself. He felt a strange prickle of remorse and wondered how the farm was doing these days, and how Hoskuld was faring, bereft of the sword that carried his family's honour.

But it was a thought he did not wish to dwell on. He shook himself. 'Anyway,' he said dismissively, 'the men all speak of its richness – they too recognise good land when they see it.'

'They do,' agreed his father. 'They look down on it from the walls with hungry eyes and urge me to share it out.'

'Then why don't you? Is it not ours for the taking?'

Ivar shook his head. 'Taking and holding are two very different things. We are not masters here yet. We have taken York, but we have not yet defended it. When we have crushed the power of the Northumbrian fyrd and sent both kings to Odin, then it will be time for sharing out land. Until then we must content ourselves with raiding halls and plundering monasteries.'

But how long would that take? Sigfrid wanted action. He turned to study the new defences Ivar had built over the past five months. They were formidable. The old walls surrounding the town had been reinforced and a smaller wooden stockade built inside them, enclosing the moot hall and the Christian holy place – the *mynster*, the Saxons called it. On the town bank of the river Foss, more ramparts and earthworks had been thrown up to create a safe harbour for the ships. Sigfrid smiled. They were ready for anything. 'I cannot understand why we have been left so long unchallenged,' he said.

His father laughed. 'Because the two kings had first to convince themselves that they hated us more than they hated each other. But we shall not be left in peace much longer. My spies tell me a truce has been agreed and an army is even now gathering to march on York.'

'Good,' said Sigfrid. 'They will be in for a shock. This place must be impregnable by now.'

'No, not impregnable. There are still weaknesses in the old wall.'

'But we will strengthen them?'

'No. It is part of my plan to leave them as they are.'

'What!'

'War is not always won by the sword alone, Sigfrid. Sometimes it takes cunning and deception. What is seen as a weakness can really be a strength.'

'But how ...' Sigfrid was dumbfounded. 'I don't understand.'

'You will,' promised Ivar, laughing, 'You will.'

🙂 🙂 🙂

The monastery at Lastingham sat like a fortress among the windswept hills of the North Deira moors. The historian, Bede, had once described its location as 'a place more suitable for the dens of robbers and haunts of wild beasts than for human habitation'. In winter the north wind howled around its walls like a hungry wolf, freezing the water in the fishponds and crippling the hands of the monks in the scriptorium, until their aching fingers could no longer hold their pens. Even now, on this evening in late March, it swept savagely across the moors from the north-east, driving before it a cold, thin, needle-sharp drizzle of sleet.

The man struggling up the path towards its gates wondered how anyone could possibly choose to live in such a spot. But at the same time he thanked God for its isolation. Its very remoteness promised safety, and at this moment that was the only thing that mattered to him. He drew the hood of his cloak more tightly about his face and bent his head into the driving sleet, dragging himself on leaden feet towards the security of its walls.

At last his hand touched the frayed bell-rope hanging beside the gate. He pulled it and a deep clanging tone echoed startlingly above the howl of the wind. After a while, a small, barred shutter in the door was drawn back and a face peered out at him. It studied him for a moment, then, apparently satisfied that he was harmless, disappeared again. With a great rattling of chains and scraping of bolts the door was opened. The man slipped inside and stood shivering in the shelter of the little gatehouse.

The porter surveyed the weary figure and, indicating the brazier in the centre of the room, said sympathetically, 'Rest here, friend, and warm yourself. Then I will take you to the hospice. You have come from York?'

The man nodded. He lowered himself onto a bench near the brazier and leaned forward, stretching his hands out to the heat. Steam rose in a cloud from his sodden garments and permeated the room with the smell of damp wool. For some moments he sat without moving, then he looked up and said abruptly, 'Fetch the abbot to me.'

The porter looked surprised, but he had been trained always to treat guests with courtesy so he merely said gently, 'I'm afraid that is not possible at the moment. The Lord Abbot is in chapel with all the brothers. It is the hour of prayer.'

'I don't care where he is or what hour it is. I need to speak to him urgently. Fetch him to me.'

The porter hesitated. He was a novice – barely seventeen years old – and in an agony of indecision. In a monastery, the hours of prayer were sacrosanct. To drag the abbot from chapel merely to interview another fugitive from York would surely be a grave sin; yet there was something about the visitor that demanded obedience. It was hard to see what he looked like under his thick, dark cloak, but the clasp that pinned that cloak, the rings adorning his fingers and the soft, fine-grained, leather boots on his feet all suggested rank and authority. Eventually the young man murmured, 'Very well, my Lord,' and went to do his bidding.

When he returned a few minutes later with his predictably irate superior, the visitor was still sitting by the fire, but he had taken off his cloak and when he turned towards them, they were both able to get a proper look at him. The abbot gasped and ran forward. He dropped to his knees at the man's side. 'My Lord, the king, forgive me. I was not told it was you.' He whirled around on his bewildered novice. 'Well, don't stand there gawping, brother. Do you not recognise the Lord Aelle? Go immediately and see that a suitable room is made ready for him and have the cooks prepare food and drink.'

The young man scuttled off and soon the exhausted Aelle found himself sitting by a fire in the best guest room, sipping mulled wine and polishing off a large grilled carp. He leaned back with a sigh. 'That's better,' he said. 'I have been on the road for five days, travelling by night and hiding like a frightened hare by day. I have eaten nothing for two days.'

The abbot nodded. 'It was that bad?' he asked sympathetically.

'It was butchery! We allowed them to deceive us. We attacked the wall where we knew the defences to be weakest. They fell back before us and we thought we had broken them. Half the fyrd had followed them through the breach in the wall before we discovered the truth. It was a trap. They had built another, inner fortress and we were caught between the two lines of defence. They fought like fiends out of hell. We were driven back and as we tried to get out, the rest of the fyrd, not understanding what had happened, was trying to get in.' He shuddered. 'It was butchery,' he repeated. 'Like the slaughtering of cattle. Osbert is dead; I saw him fall. God alone knows how I managed to escape. My hearthtroop closed around me and somehow they forced a passage for me, but it will have cost them their lives, every one of them.' He put his head in his hands, overwhelmed by the memory.

'God will reward them,' said the abbot gently. He sighed. 'Osbert's hearth companions were not so valiant, it seems. I have one of them here, his nephew, Egbert. He arrived seeking sanctuary two days ago.'

'Egbert?' The king looked up and his lip curled into a sneer. 'That does not surprise me. I know him of old. He would have been the first to run.' He thought for a moment. 'Well, since he is here, he can make himself useful to me.'

'My Lord?'

'I need someone to carry a message to Bishop Wulf-here. Like it or not, we are going to have to come to terms with these barbarians, and I shall need his counsel. Thank God he was not in York when they captured it.'

'Thank God, indeed,' agreed the abbot. 'Very well, I will have Egbert sent to you first thing in the morning.

But now you must rest, my Lord. You are worn out from your ordeal.'

Aelle was only too thankful to comply.

☙ ☙ ☙

'I will not do it!' said Egbert. 'They have warbands out all over the countryside, hunting down survivors. It would be like putting a knife to my own throat.'

'You will do it,' said his king. 'For if you do not, *I* will put a knife to your throat! Your uncle brought down this affliction on us all the day he took these barbarians into his pay. Now, since you wouldn't defend his life, you can defend his memory by helping me make peace with them. Bishop Wulfhere is at Ripon, or he was when last I had news of him. You will ride there and bring him back with you.'

'Ripon!' Egbert's heart sank. Ripon was a good two days' journey away across the Vale of York, a countryside that would be crawling with Viking war bands. 'And what if he is not there?' he demanded.

'Then you will find out where he is and follow him.'

'But he may have been captured! What if the Vikings have already plundered the place?'

'You will find him,' repeated Aelle, remorselessly. 'Or you will die in the attempt.'

'No,' protested Egbert, but it was a waste of breath. An

hour later, in a borrowed cloak and riding the abbot's own horse, he found himself wending his way down out of the hills. He turned westward, skirting the edge of the moors. His mind still seethed with indignation. This was a gross injustice. Why should he be expected to risk his neck for Aelle? Aelle was not his Lord. He was not even the rightful king. He had stolen the title from Osbert. If there had been any way out, anywhere left for him to run to ... but there wasn't. Egbert was also a fugitive. After the debacle at York he was the only surviving legitimate heir to the Northumbrian kingship. If the Vikings didn't kill him, then Aelle probably would, eventually. Unless ...

An idea flickered in his mind – a wild, hugely dangerous idea – but one that might give him the only chance he was ever likely to have of saving his life. He turned it over, looked at it from every angle, and was still weighing the odds when he came to where an ancient road cut across his track. He drew rein and looked about him. He was in familiar territory. Ten miles to the south lay York, Ripon was fifteen miles west, while close at hand, hidden by a bend in the road, lay the monastery of Crayke. He knew the place well, for he had often enjoyed its hospitality, stopping for a meal or to seek a night's shelter on his journeys through the vale. He decided to call there now. The abbot would help him; he was no friend of Aelle's and no great admirer of Bishop Wulfhere. Together they would discuss the situation and consider his next move.

He rounded the bend and hope shrivelled to a walnut-sized lump in his belly. There would be no welcome for him at Crayke today. Others had been that way before him and all that was left of the place was the blackened skeleton of the chapel, raising charred limbs to the sky in silent agony.

'No!' Egbert let out a howl of rage and anguish. Damn Aelle! Damn his black soul to everlasting torment! This outrage was a horror of his making. In his greed and hunger for power, he had split the kingdom and opened the door for these barbarians. Well, let the usurper pay the price for it. His own mind was made up. With a savage jerk on the reins he turned his horse around and headed southward.

☻ ☻ ☻

Life at Lastingham followed the rhythm of the monastery bell. From matins until compline it called the brothers to their prayers and measured the hours of their work and recreation. It was not an easy life. Only the truly dedicated man would rise each day before dawn to spend hours kneeling on the damp floor of an icy chapel, or sit from morning 'til night hunched over pages of vellum in a draughty scriptorium. But if the discipline was hard, the peace and tranquility that went with it were more easily appreciated. To the weary and dispirited Aelle, Lastingham soon came to feel like an ark of sanity in a world turned upside down by bloodshed and terror.

As his health and courage returned, he even began to anticipate with growing confidence his coming negotiations with the Viking, Ivar. After all, he reasoned, the Dane was a barbarian; he, Aelle, was almost certainly more intelligent, and a past-master in the art of bargaining. He knew this country, Ivar didn't. He had skills and experience to offer. He would not be greedy. He would merely ask for the same terms Ivar had once offered Edmund of East Anglia. And he would accept, with a great show of gratitude. Afterwards ... well that was a different matter. There would be time later for duplicity. He had something to offer, too – a hostage – the last remaining heir of Osbert's line. He smiled as the thought occurred to him. Yes, he would hand Egbert over to Ivar to do with as he pleased. It was an arrangement that would probably suit them both. With these thoughts in his mind he began to sleep more easily, freed from the nightmares that had haunted him since the massacre at York.

The attack came early in the morning – a thunder of hooves, a pounding in of the gate, a mob that swept through the cloisters like a pack of wolves, howling, tearing, killing anything that got in their way. The house of God was turned into a slaughter house. The chapel was ransacked, the tabernacle torn open, consecrated hosts scattered and trampled on the floor. Barns and store rooms were ripped apart for plunder. Sheep, cattle, chickens, even valuable horses, were butchered simply for the sport of it and anything that would burn was put to the torch in an orgy of vandalism.

And then it was the turn of the inhabitants. Those young and fit enough to fetch a price in the Dublin slave market were dragged out into the courtyard to be chained and taken back to York. The old and infirm were dispatched on the spot. Aelle had fled to the infirmary, but even this sanctuary was not respected. The Vikings smashed the door in with swords and axes and he was quickly dragged out and dumped beside the rest of the survivors. He lay in the mud that had been churned up by milling feet, bruised and bloodied and consumed with terror. This could not be happening! But the sobs and screams were real enough and so were the shaggy figures milling around him and the gruff Scandinavian voices.

Another voice, a light English voice, made itself heard above the din. 'That one, that man there – let me see his face.'

Aelle found himself dragged to his knees. A hand seized his hair and jerked his head up. He blinked upwards. Elegant, arrogant, still wearing his borrowed cloak, Egbert grinned down at him from the saddle of the abbot's horse. 'This is the man you want,' he said with a spiteful laugh. 'This is the man who likes to call himself King of Northumbria.'

Rage finally overcame Aelle's fear. He wrenched himself free and flung himself at his betrayer with murderous determination. The Vikings closed around him. He went down under a hail of kicks and blows. Something solid smacked him over the head and he heard a voice shout, 'Don't kill him. Remember, we have to take him back alive.' He passed out.

One of the raiders picked up his inert body and threw it over the back of a horse. Soon a grim procession was winding its way through the gate and out onto the bleakness of the moors. Behind them, rising in a thick pall from the burning ruins, a cloud of smoke hung over the monastery, a cloud as black as the shadow of a raven.

12

SECRETS OF THE RUNES

It had been an act of sheer inspiration, thought Sigfrid, to choose the mynster as the place of sacrifice. What more effective seal could Ivar set on his conquest of Northumbria than to offer its king to Odin on the altar of his own White Christ? He glanced admiringly at his father. Today, in this holy place of the Saxons, Ivar shone with a barbaric splendour. Last night he had prepared himself. In a specially built bathhouse he had sweated the grime from his body and Sigfrid had helped him scrub his skin until it glowed. His hair was washed, his beard trimmed, his chain-mail byrnie had been polished until it gleamed like ice. His eyes glittered with an otherworldly light, as if they looked into the heart of Asgard. Today he was more than a warrior. He was the shaman – the priest-king of his people – come to offer sacrifice.

What a pity though, that so few of those present seemed to share this sense of solemnity. Ubbe understood. The runemaster was his usual enigmatic self. But as for the others ... why, even Halfdan, Sigfrid suspected, had only come for the entertainment and would as cheerfully have dedicated their victim to his own White Christ, if that had promised better sport.

Sigfrid felt a twinge of uneasiness, but Ivar seemed unbothered by the lack of awe. He turned to his brothers. 'Fetch me the offering,' he ordered.

When the two men returned with their victim, Sigfrid's heart sank. Battered, bedraggled, trussed like a yuletide goose, Aelle was not an imposing sight. His face was grey, his eyes half mad with terror. When they dropped him to the floor, he squirmed like a headless snake, and made incomprehensible moaning sounds in the back of his throat.

'*When you give a man to Odin; when you look into his eyes and know that he sees his death written in your own ...*' Sigfrid looked into the eyes of Aelle of Northumbria. Gods of Asgard, was this the moment he had dreamed of? Was this pathetic creature really their sacred offering, the conduit for the great truth his father had promised him? Why, he might as well have been at a bear-baiting. He turned in disgust and would have walked from the mynster, but into his mind crept a sudden memory – another time, another place, a golden giant who had looked down on him from the saddle of his horse. No, it didn't have to be like this. He touched his sword. *You have been cheated, Lord Odin. We have both been cheated. This man is not worthy of you. But one day, one day, with your help …*

'Prepare the sacrifice,' Ivar commanded.

Halfdan cut the thong that bound Aelle's wrists and stripped him of his tunic and undershirt. Then he and Ubbe dragged him to the altar and held him pinned against it. Aelle was still on his knees, his face was pressed against the stone, his arms outstretched in a parody of the White Christ on his cross. He howled and struggled unavailingly. Ivar came to stand behind him. He drew his sword and the blade with its jewelled hilt flashed fire in the encircling candlelight. He raised it above his head.

'Now I give thee to Odin,' he said. And his arm swept downward.

Aelle's screams penetrated every corner of the mynster.

✾ ✾ ✾

'But you promised me,' insisted Sigfrid. 'You promised me two years ago. How much longer must I wait?' He set his drinking horn down with a thump and looked to his uncles for support. Neither of them spoke.

'I know I promised you,' agreed his father. 'And I do not break my word. But there is a time to fight and a time to rest and consolidate. True vengeance does not cool from waiting.'

'Waiting! It is in my mind that is all we ever do, these days. For over a year now we have been masters of North-umbria and we sit here like sheep in a meadow, content in our idleness. Your warriors are turning into farmers. If we wait much longer you will have no one left to follow you.'

His father laughed. 'They followed me to Nottingham readily enough last winter.'

'Aye. And followed you back again in the spring, with their tails between their legs.'

'What!'

Before Sigfrid could think or defend himself, a fist crashed into his face and sent him sprawling on the ground. Ivar stood over him. 'You dare to say this!' he roared. 'Get up, you whining puppy. Get up and defend your insolence. You throw your weight around like a man; let's see if you can fight like one.'

Sigfrid stumbled to his feet. His head rang from the blow, his mind reeled from the suddenness and savagery of it. He felt sick and scared. This time he had really gone too far. 'Forgive me, father,' he mumbled. 'I'm sorry, I'm sorry.' He backed away and, dropping his hands to his sides, turned the hands palm outward in a gesture of submission. Ivar raised his fist again, but Ubbe stepped between them. 'Stop this,' he said. 'The boy is at fault, but do you want the whole world to see you fighting?'

'He called me a coward. In my own hall, he accused me of cowardice.'

'Aye, and who but a true son of yours would be rash or brave enough? There is no malice in the boy, Ivar. He has your courage, but not yet your wisdom. He spoke out of youth and thoughtlessness. Didn't you, Sigfrid?'

'Yes,' said Sigfrid. His mind was spinning in panic. He didn't really think his father would kill him, but what would he do if Ivar threw him out? Where would he go? To Dublin? Impossible without his father's blessing. To Denmark, where he was wanted as a thief and possibly an outlaw? To Norway or Sweden, to spend the rest of his life among strangers? What had he done, in one moment of stupidity? He dropped to his knees and raised clasped hands to his father. 'My Lord, father, forgive me, I did not mean the words I said. My life is yours. You know it is. I crossed the seas to find you. I would follow you to the ends of the earth if need be. My tongue may have failed you, but my heart and my sword arm never will.'

There was an agonising silence during which he did

not dare to raise his eyes. Then Ivar took the clasped hands between his own. 'So,' he said heavily, 'I forgive you, but learn to bridle that tongue of yours, for if it turns traitor again I will cut it out. Now go, and do not come back to the hall until I send for you, when my temper has had time to cool.'

Sigfrid didn't wait to be told twice. He retreated to an ale house in the town to contemplate his narrow escape, and was still sitting there when Ubbe came looking for him some time later.

Ubbe was not sympathetic. 'Do you realise what you nearly did, you little fool?' he demanded angrily. 'Do you realise that, had you been any other man, we would even now be preparing your funeral?'

Sigfrid nodded miserably. 'Will he ever truly forgive me, do you think?'

'You must ask him that yourself. But, yes, I think he will. You are his son, and he admires your spirit, if not your recklessness. An arrogance that might bring death to another man may be boasted of in one's own flesh and blood.'

'Am I arrogant?'

'All young men are arrogant. It is no bad thing in itself, but you must learn when to curb it.'

'I shall,' said Sigfrid with feeling. 'Believe me, I shall.'

It was several days before he summoned up the

courage to approach his father again. Ivar received him sternly. 'I hope you have learned your lesson,' he said. 'Had you been any other man's son, I would have killed you where you stood.'

'And I would have deserved it,' agreed Sigfrid humbly. 'But, father, had I been any other man's son, would I have been born with your temper or your pride?' He looked Ivar full in the face. The Viking was silent for a moment, then he laughed.

'By the Gods!' he chuckled. 'I did a good day's work the day I married your mother. You are a son to be proud of. But Ubbe was right, although you have my courage you have not yet my wisdom. Did you really think it was fear prevented me from giving battle at Nottingham last winter?'

'No, but ...'

'We overstretched ourselves, invading Mercia so soon after taking York. We were penned in at Nottingham – you saw how it was – we could not get out, and the Saxons were not strong enough to break in. Victory is not always won by feats of arms. In the end it was cunning won the day. Do you know how much gold they gave us to leave peacefully?'

Sigfrid nodded. 'I do. And we needed it. Armies have to be paid, I can understand that, but ...'

'But you are restless. Your sword seeks blood again?'

'It seeks truth. I did not find it here.'

Ivar looked at him thoughtfully. 'It did not satisfy you, then, the king-sacrifice?'

'It was a travesty. What use to Odin a shrieking, grovelling coward?'

'Aelle was a king. It is the act that counts, not the spectacle. All men lose their courage sooner or later in the claws of the bloodeagle.'

'No,' said Sigfrid softly. 'No, not all.'

He lapsed into silence. For a moment Ivar too was silent. Then he smiled. 'So, that is how the land lies, eh? Well, you may have your chance sooner than you think. Despite your accusations, I have not been idle all these months. My preparations are almost complete. Only one thing now is lacking and tomorrow night ...'

'Yes?' Sigfrid's heart leapt expectantly.

'Tomorrow night, when the moon is full, Ubbe will cast the runes.'

The makeshift gallows creaked beneath its burden and the sound carried harshly on the still night air. The body had ceased to kick some time ago. It swung gently, turning as it moved and its sightless eyes stared out over the heads of the four men crouched at the foot of the scaffold. They spared it hardly a glance. The man had been a thrall, chosen for his strength and physical beauty.

Ubbe had spread his cloak beneath the gallows and on it a lighted wick flickered in a bowl of tallow. Its small light was sufficient, under a full moon, for the business in hand. Now he rose, and, standing before the swinging corpse, stretched his arms skyward. 'All-father, Odin, who hung nine days upon the tree of life to gain the secrets of the runes, accept the sacrifice I offer you and give me wisdom to read wisely the messages they bring tonight.'

He unfastened the goatskin pouch at his belt, and, loosening the drawstring, scattered the contents onto the cloak – fifteen squares of ash bark, each inscribed with a single runic character. Discarding those that had fallen face downwards, he squatted on his heels and surveyed the remainder slowly and thoughtfully. Sigfrid watched him, wondering what he saw, what message there might be for himself in these mysterious symbols, and whether, if he asked Ubbe to teach him, the gift of divination might ever be given to him.

The silence lengthened, then at last Ubbe shook himself as if coming out of a dream and eased himself into a more comfortable position. 'So,' he said, 'the runes speak to us.'

'And?' demanded Ivar.

His brother smiled and held up a hand. 'Slowly, slowly. First name me your own sign among these pieces.'

'This one,' said Ivar, pointing without hesitation.

'Tiawaz, the warrior's rune, it has to be.'

'Tiawaz the warrior,' confirmed Ubbe. 'Yes, that is well chosen. And see where it lies, close to the front of the display. Now, look here,' he motioned with his hand. 'You see this piece above Tiawaz? That is Nauthiz, the rune of the Norns. It is promising, very promising. It means the weavers of destiny, Fate, Being and Necessity, hold you under their protection.'

'I knew it,' said Ivar triumphantly.

'But there is more. See this one here? This shows where you stand tonight – your hopes, your fears, the questions you would ask.'

'But that is the ice rune,' said Ivar, and he frowned. 'The rune of standstill and frustration, perhaps even signifying the end of a journey.'

Ubbe chuckled. 'Ah, yes, but the end of one journey can mean the beginning of another. This is also the rune of Ymir the frost giant, from whose body was formed the world of men. True, it is the rune of discontent, but out of it great things may grow.'

'And what about this one?' It was Halfdan's turn to touch one of the squares. 'Even I know this one. It is Uruz, the rune of courage and manhood.'

'You are right, Halfdan. And it is a rune of great power. It represents man in all his glory, his strength, his physical beauty, his nobility. Placed where it is tonight, it represents the future, the answer you have come to seek.' He glanced at Ivar and then at Sigfrid. 'This rune,' he said, 'is the symbol of the aurochs – the wild bull, the sacrificial offering.'

'Oh!' Sigfrid caught his breath. He looked at his father and Ivar grinned back at him.

'Odin smiles on us,' said the Viking. He lifted his head, his eyes gazing above the body on the gallows. 'Hear me, Lord Odin. Bring success to this campaign, and before the year is out you shall have a gift greater than any I have ever offered you.'

'The runes decree it,' said Ubbe. He reached to gather them up, but Sigfrid stopped him. 'Wait,' he said. 'There is one more here you have not explained. What does this one mean?'

'Nothing,' said his uncle, a little too hastily. He swept the bark squares back into the bag and secured it at his belt. 'Nothing. It fell too far from the others to have any bearing on them.'

'But what was it? I am curious.'

Ubbe hesitated for a long while, then, 'It was the rune of Loki,' he said reluctantly. 'But as I explained, it was too far from the others to affect them.'

He was lying. Sigfrid knew it. Their success lay under a cloud. Loki was the God of mischief and deceit, a God whose malice could twist the very workings of fate.

Under Odin's banner they would have victory in East Anglia, but Loki might still somehow bring it tumbling down about their shoulders.

Nobody else seemed worried by the possibility, or perhaps they just didn't want to think about it. Ivar made final plans for the invasion. They would split their army. Ivar and Halfdan would travel with the ships, taking Sigfrid with them, while Ubbe would lead a mounted warband back through Mercia. Egbert, the traitorous young Saxon, was to be left as a puppet-king in York, to hold Northumbria until their return.

'So,' said Sigfrid, when his father outlined his plans to him. 'It is in your mind then to return afterwards and settle in York?'

'No,' said Ivar. 'I am still the King of Dublin. Halfdan can have York, or perhaps …' He looked sideways at his son. Sigfrid shook his head.

'No, father. I meant what I said. You are my Lord and where you go, I follow.'

Ivar looked inordinately pleased. 'Then when we have concluded our business with King Edmund, we shall winter in East Anglia before …' he grinned. 'I have had further messages from Olaf. He grows restless in Pictland and talks of a raid on the kingdom of Strathclyde. What would you say to joining forces with him there before returning to Ireland?'

'I would say "yes",' said Sigfrid. This was the first time Ivar had invited his opinion and the recognition thrilled him to the core. It also made him bold. 'Father,' he ventured, 'I have a favour to ask of you.'

'Ask it, then.'

'A big favour.'

'I am listening.'

Sigfrid drew a deep breath. 'Remember when we first met? When you called me Sigfrid TruthSeeker and looked at my sword and told me it was the weapon of a king?'

Ivar nodded.

'You said something else as well. You said, *"When you give a man to Odin at the point of your sword. When you look into his eyes and know that he sees his death written in your own, that is the moment when you will understand the meaning of victory."*'

'Did I?' said Ivar. 'And?'

'And, ever since, I have been seeking that truth – that knowledge. But I have not found it. It was not in Aelle's eyes, nor in those of any man I have killed in battle. There is only one man who can give it to me and I want … I want …'

He broke off, unnerved by the enormity of his request. Ivar studied him.

'I know what you want, Sigfrid TruthSeeker,' he said

softly. 'How old are you now, truthfully?'

'I was nineteen on my last birthday.'

'So, a man, then, and a warrior. Very well, then, you shall have your wish. When we have defeated the East Anglians, you shall put your sword to the back of their king, and offer him to Odin.'

13

FIRST BLOOD

Through spring and summer the breckland around Thetford had been a blaze of colour: golden gorse, the deep purple of ling and the more delicate shades of milk-vetch and maiden pink. But today, even the last of the heather had gone. Curlews cried across bare, wind-swept heath and the breckland meres – huge puddles that would disappear again with the end of winter – reflected only the grey clouds above them and the skeletons of a few sparse stands of beech.

Across this bleak landscape, the two armies made camp almost within sight of each other. Edmund stood with

Ulfkytel before his tent as the sun went down, watching the flickering lights of the myriad small campfires around which the East Anglian fyrd was settling down for the night. A red glow in the distance suggested that, behind their own lines, his enemies were similarly engaged.

'I wonder how well Ubbe will sleep tonight?' said Ulfkytel, breaking across his thoughts. 'He is not used to fighting on his own.'

Edmund frowned. 'I know,' he said. 'But where is Ivar? Why is he not with his brother? What game is he playing?'

'Perhaps he dare not turn his back on Northumbria. Or maybe he thinks us weak and not worthy of his personal attention.'

'No.' Edmund could not believe that. He remembered the way Ivar had looked at him at their last parting. 'No, he has a score to settle. He would not let others do it for him.'

'Well, whatever his reasons, I am not complaining. *Sufficient unto the day are the evils thereof.* The enemy is before us and tomorrow we shall fight him. There will be time enough afterwards for worrying about any other plans he may be hatching.'

He was right, of course, but Edmund could not dismiss the matter so easily. Something else was afoot, something he should know about.

A youth came over from the fire with a jug of mulled ale and two drinking horns. He poured for the men and stood watching them while they drank. 'It is so quiet,' he said at last. 'I had not thought it would be so quiet.'

'The calm before the storm,' said Edmund. 'Are you afraid, Leofstan?'

His young armour-bearer looked startled. 'Of course not,' he said indignantly, but his eyes told another tale.

Edmund smiled at him. 'There is no shame in fear. You will fight all the better for it. But you should be in your bed, we shall all be up again at first light.'

'I would not be able to sleep, my Lord. With your permission I would like to remain here a while.'

His eyes pleaded eloquently. Edmund nodded. 'Very well, then, but fetch yourself a drinking horn. If you are to share our vigil, then you should also share our ale.'

'Oh … thank you, my Lord.' With a surprised gasp the boy shot off to do as he was bidden.

Ulfkytel chuckled. 'He will boast of this for the rest of his life – the night he was invited to drink with his king. And if he dies tomorrow he will consider it a small price to pay for such an honour.'

'Then he is a fool. By this time tomorrow we may all be dead, and a corpse is neither king nor commoner. Ah, Ulfkytel, I did not want this fight. He is so young. They are all so young.'

'Twenty-eight summers have hardly made you a grey-beard yourself, my Lord. And the fight was none of your making. Your men love you. There is not one of them would wish himself anywhere else tonight.'

'Then I can only pray they have not changed their minds by this time tomorrow.'

Leofstan returned with his drinking horn. Ulfkytel filled it for him, grinning into the lad's awe-struck face. He raised his own vessel. 'To you, my young warrior. May you cover yourself in glory and live to tell the tale to your grandchildren.'

'To victory,' said Edmund. And they drank.

As the first fingers of dawn crept across the eastern sky, Bishop Humbert said mass for them. The old man had insisted on accompanying the fyrd to Thetford. 'At my age, I am not long for this world anyway,' he had said when Edmund tried to dissuade him. 'And could I face my God knowing I had deserted my king in his hour of greatest need?'

Despite his concerns for the old man's safety, Edmund was grateful for his presence. He watched as Humbert raised first the host then the chalice in the act of consecration and found himself listening with new awareness to the familiar words. 'Hoc ist enim calix sanguine mei' – *This is the chalice of my blood.* How much blood would be spilt before this day was out? *Oh, Christ, who died on the cross to save mankind, grant that those who die for you today may find peace in your everlasting mercy.*

The mass had scarcely ended when a scout galloped up to warn them that the Danes were on the move. Edmund climbed to the top of the rise to observe them. They advanced in a great tidal wave, blowing horns and chanting their pagan war-cries. Edmund tried to estimate their strength and to his relief realised that at least he would not be outnumbered. He turned to Ulfkytel and they smiled at each other, hard, mirthless smiles. Edmund nodded his head.

Ulfkytel blew a long blast on his horn and instantly the camp was astir. Men grabbed their weapons, thanes rallied their followers, everyone moved swiftly to his assigned position. They waited. The Vikings had halted just out of bowshot and were working themselves up for the attack. They stood behind a wall of locked shields, yelling, jeering, banging their swords against the lindenwood and bellowing obscene insults at their foes.

'Don't let them shake you,' Edmund had ordered. 'We occupy the higher ground. Hold fast. Make them come to us.' His fyrd obeyed him. Through a barrage of abuse they stood firm and unresponsive. Finally the Danes lost patience. They began to advance again and as soon as they were within range, the East Anglian bowmen loosed a torrent of arrows. The Viking army broke into a run, attempting to close the gap before the archers could do too much damage, and at last Edmund gave the signal. A roar went up all along the East Anglian lines and the whole fyrd poured down the hill and closed with the enemy.

Once the two sides locked, it was every man for himself. The battle-line writhed to and fro across the heath like a monstrous serpent, but for each warrior it was a personal struggle: the man before him, the weapon in his hand, the relentlessly repeated ordeal of single combat. Edmund came in for ferocious attention, but his hearthtroop closed around him like a wall. If one man fell, another stepped into the breach and his standard, held proudly by Leofstan, never dipped or faltered. It was ironic, thought Edmund, in the few moments he had time for lucid thought, that this spot in the very thick of the fighting was probably the safest place for the boy in his first battle.

The body count rose sickeningly. The ground underfoot grew slippery with blood. The sun climbed, reached its zenith and began its fall towards the west. And still the two armies continued to pound each other. The fighting was sporadic, for no man can sustain indefinitely the rigours of single combat. Opposing groups would batter each other into exhaustion, then retreat as if by common consent to recover, regroup and proceed to batter one another again.

In the confusion it was difficult to make out who was

winning, but by mid afternoon Edmund thought he detected an encouraging swing. He had withdrawn with his bodyguard from a particularly long and gruelling skirmish and was observing the conflict from the safety of a small hill. 'They are giving ground,' he rejoiced. 'Look, we are pushing them back towards the river.' He leaned on his sword and sucked in great lungfuls of air. He was exhausted, his head thumped like a butter churn and his sword arm felt as though it was encased in lead. But this was no time for resting. 'We must go down again,' he urged, 'press home our advantage before they have a chance to rally.'

Leofstan put a hand on his shoulder. 'My Lord, there is no need. You have done enough. See, they are breaking and the lord Ulfkytel is rallying your hearthtroop to finish them off. He will drive them from the field.'

It was true, or partly true. The Danes were not broken, but they clearly realised they had no hope now of carrying the day. With as much dignity as they could maintain, they were retreating to a more easily defended position across the river. But the East Anglians were too tired and too few in number to pursue them safely into the gathering darkness. The fyrd must be warned against rashness. 'Go down onto the field,' Edmund commanded Leofstan. 'Seek out the Lord Ulfkytel and warn him against headlong pursuit. Tell him to see our wounded brought in safely and then join me in my tent. We must plan ahead. We may have to fight again tomorrow.'

Leofstan sped off to carry out his orders and Edmund retired to his tent. He tried to give thanks for the victory, but it was not one to inspire great rejoicing. The cost in Saxon life had been appalling, and there was no certainty the Danes would not attack again in the morning. He was bone-tired and the thought of having to go through today's horrors all over again was mind-numbing. He longed for Humbert's reassuring presence, but the bishop would be busy elsewhere, comforting the wounded and dying. He would have to go down and visit them himself later. For now, he would wait for Ulfkytel and a full report.

It was some time later that he heard shouts and running footsteps. The tent flap burst open and Leofstan stood in the doorway. His eyes were wild and he was gasping for breath. 'My Lord, my Lord, you must come quickly!'

'What is it, boy?'

'The Lord Ulfkytel ... a Danish arrow... in the chest. They have taken him to Bishop Humbert's tent. They say ...'

He broke down, covering his face with his hands. Edmund gripped him by the shoulders. 'What do they say? Tell me, Leofstan.'

'They say he is dying, my Lord.'

Dying? Ulfkytel? Tough, laughing unassailable Ulfkytel, who had been his friend, his brother almost, since earliest childhood. It couldn't be. It wasn't possible.

Ulfkytel lay on a pallet in Humbert's quarters, on a sheet already soaked through with his blood. His head and shoulders were raised on cushions. An arrow protruded from his chest. His eyes were closed, his breath came in long, rattling gasps, his skin was clammy, and had the faint, blue translucence of watered milk.

Humbert was kneeling by his side. He looked up as Edmund came in and shook his head in answer to the king's unspoken question. 'I have given him the last rites,' he said. 'There is little more any of us can do. He has lost too much blood.'

Edmund moved closer to the bed. Ulfkytel seemed to sense his presence. His eyelids flickered and opened. 'Edmund?'

'Yes.'

'Am I ...?'

No! words of reassurance sprang to Edmund's lips, but he thought better of them. This was no time for lies. He leaned forward and took his friend's hand. 'You are dying,' he said gently.

There was a silence, broken only by the laboured

breathing. Then Ulfkytel's hand scrabbled feebly across his chest to touch the arrow.

'Please ... not like this.'

'You wish me to remove it?'

'Yes.'

Humbert shook his head, but Edmund ignored him. Leaving the arrow where it was might prolong the inevitable but it would not save his friend's life and if Ulfkytel wanted it out then so be it. He summoned men to help him. Ulfkytel gasped as they snapped the arrow. He cried out, a long bubbling moan of pain, as it was withdrawn, but afterwards he smiled weakly and moved his lips in a silent thank you. Edmund sent everyone away and, taking his friend's hand between his own, settled down to his vigil.

The night dragged on remorselessly. Candle wicks flickered in their bowls of tallow, logs crumbled to ashes in the brazier. Ulfkytel did not move or speak. His eyes remained closed; he looked like one already dead. But his chest continued to rise and fall, and as each rattling sigh faded into silence Edmund found himself holding his own breath and willing his friend to take the next.

At last, just as the first rays of light crept into the tent, a change came over the still figure on the bed. Ulfkytel stirred. His eyes fluttered open. His hand jerked as if to pull free from Edmund's grasp.

Edmund leaned forward. 'Ulfkytel?'

'Let me go.'

'What?'

'I'm tired, Edmund, let me go.'

'No.' For a moment Edmund clung still harder. Every instinct in him fought against surrender, but at last he relinquished his grip. 'Go in peace,' he said.

Ulfkytel closed his eyes. He was still for a long moment, then he opened them again. They seemed to stare at something over Edmund's shoulder. His chest heaved, he retched twice, a bubble of blood trickled from his mouth. It was over.

Edmund sat for a long moment without moving. Then he leaned forward and closed Ulfkytel's eyes. With his thumb he traced the sign of the cross on his friend's forehead. Then he rose and went out into the dawn.

On the battlefield they were burying the enemy, tumbling the bodies into pits and flinging dirt over them. Edmund looked down at his fallen foes. In death there seemed nothing very terrible about them, nothing to mark them out as the barbarians who had just killed his lifelong friend. Their faces might almost have been Saxon. That man there – the one with those blue, staring, dead eyes – for a moment he half thought he recognised him. But no, Ivar's son would be eighteen now, nineteen at the most? This was a warrior in his middle twenties.

It was a handsome face, strangely gentle in death. It had belonged to a living man, somebody's son, somebody's lover, probably somebody's father. Yesterday, this man had been alive. He had laughed, joked, marched with his companions, boasted about the glory he would win. Now, he was dead. Killed by a single blow that appeared to have broken his neck without even gashing the skin.

Such stupid, such senseless, such unnecessary waste. A wave of anger swept over Edmund, and, falling to his knees, he cried, over the body of his unknown enemy, the tears he had been unable to shed for Ulfkytel. It left him drained, but oddly cleansed. He stood up. There were matters to be seen to, plans to be made. The Danes had retreated further during the night, but who knew when they might rally again? The fyrd must be rested and reprovisioned. Uylfkytel's body must be taken back to Hellesdon for burial. He must promote a new leader to his hearthtroop.

'My Lord, my Lord Edmund!' A voice was shouting his name. He turned to see Bishop Humbert hurrying across the heath. The old man was out of breath, his face twisted with anxiety. Edmund ran to meet him.

'Gently, Bishop, gently. What is wrong?'

'The Reeve of Diss, my Lord. The Reeve of Diss sends word to you that ...' He stopped. Edmund felt a lurch of fear. The old man drew in several shuddering breaths and started again. 'It is the ships, my Lord, Ivar and his ships. The Reeve of Diss sends word that they are on the Waveney. They have burned and pillaged their way up from the coast and are camped on a hill overlooking the river at Hoxne.'

14

FACING THE DRAGON

Another army, a hundred ships, the Reeve of Diss had estimated. That could mean as many as three thousand men, far more than the Suffolk troops could cope with. It was the end, and Edmund knew it. The battle-ravaged East Anglian fyrd would be caught between this new force and the dregs of Ubbe's army, caught and crushed like a flea between two thumbnails. Sick to the heart, he led his forces back to Hellesdon and there sat down with his councillors to discuss the new crisis. The Witan urged defiance. 'We have beaten them once, we will do it again,' declared Wulfric of

Attleborough, the man he had chosen to replace Ulfkytel as leader of his hearthtroop.

Wulfric's fellow thanes echoed his sentiments. 'We will not fail you, my Lord. We will give our lives for you.'

Edmund smiled sadly. 'I do not doubt that. You have proved your loyalty time and time again. But we must face reality. We are outnumbered, the fyrd is depleted and exhausted. We cannot fight two armies.'

'Might we yet be able to negotiate?' asked Bishop Humbert. 'They offered terms before.'

'And they would be as unacceptable to me now as they were then. I am a Christian king, Humbert – you yourself anointed me on the day of my coronation. How can I surrender my kingdom to a pagan?'

'But do they really mean to stay in East Anglia? They already have a kingdom to defend in Northumbria, and Ivar has another in Dublin. Talk to him. Find out what he wants, what he will settle for.'

'I know already what he will settle for,' said Edmund grimly, and even as the words came from his mouth he realised that it was something he had known for a long time, ever since that day, three years ago, when he and Ulfkytel had confronted Ivar in his camp at Thetford. 'There is one thing I can offer him, one thing that will satisfy his honour and put a stop to the bloodshed.'

A shocked silence fell over the room. 'No, my Lord,'

protested the bishop. 'You must not even think it.'

'Then what must I think, Humbert? What else should I do? Abandon my people? Flee into Wessex or to the Frankish court and leave them to suffer in my place? No. Ivar believes I humiliated him and he wants vengeance. If one death will satisfy him, then so be it.'

Humbert shook his head. He looked sick. 'But do you not know what they will do to you – what they did to Aelle?'

'I know,' said Edmund. He hoped his face did not betray the state of his mind.

The Witan rose as one in indignation. 'No, my Lord. We cannot let you do this thing,' protested Wulfric.

'You can, and you must.' Edmund pretended to smile. 'Even Beowulf had to face his last dragon alone.'

'Only because his hearth companions turned coward on him. We will never desert you. We will follow you into the jaws of hell, if you ask it of us.'

'But I do not ask it. Indeed, I forbid it.' He held up a hand as Wulfric opened his mouth to argue. 'We are all tired. It grows late and we are achieving nothing. Let me think further on this and we will talk again in the morning.'

'But …'

'Go. That is an order.'

Reluctantly they left him.

Bishop Humbert woke to the sound of a tap on his door.

It was still pitch dark, around midnight, he guessed. He lit a candle and shuffled across the room. 'Who is there?' he muttered, opening the door and peering out into the darkness.

'Forgive me, Humbert, for intruding on your sleep, but I need to talk to you. I need you to hear my confession.'

'Oh, dear God.' Humbert drew his King into the room and sat him down on the bed. He pulled up a stool beside him. 'Oh, Edmund. So you are really determined, then, to go through with this thing?'

Edmund nodded.

'But now? This very night?'

'I must. It has to be done, and if I leave it until morning I may not ...'

He did not finish his sentence. Humbert shuddered. He tried not to imagine what lay ahead. What gave a man this kind of courage? He wanted to plead with the king, but instinct said it was too late. 'Very well,' he said gently. 'Make your confession, my son.'

Edmund knelt. He had little of which to accuse himself: stubbornness, an occasional lack of charity, a few sins of the flesh – the simple lapses of a godfearing man. When he had finished and Humbert had given him absolution he remained on his knees for a long time. The bishop prayed he might be having second thoughts, but suddenly he looked up.

'Help me, Humbert. Give me your blessing. I am mortally afraid.'

The die was cast. With tears in his eyes, the old man laid his hands on the corn-gold head bowed before him. 'May the Lord bless thee and keep thee: may the Lord make his face shine upon thee and be gracious unto thee: may the Lord lift up his countenance to thee and give thee peace.'

He made the sign of the cross. Edmund stood up. 'God keep you, old friend.' He strode to the door and Humbert watched him helplessly.

'Edmund, wait. Please …'

Just for a moment, the young man hesitated. He turned, one hand already on the door-latch and forced his mouth into the travesty of a smile. 'You forgot to give me any penance,' he said.

The old road from Norwich to Ipswich crossed the Waveney a little east of the town of Diss. Edmund reached the ford shortly before midday. He had ridden hard – a good baffle against unwanted second thoughts – and his horse was nearly spent. Reluctantly he stopped to give it rest and water before continuing the last couple of miles to Hoxne. It was while he was sitting on the river-bank that he heard the hoofbeats. Looking up he saw a horse and rider flying down the road he had just travelled. The rider was crouched low in the saddle, galloping as if the hounds of hell were at his heels, and it was not until he reached Edmund and pulled his horse up in a lather of sweat that the king recognised him.

'Leofstan!' he said.

The boy slid from the saddle and led his mount down to the water. Then he turned and looked at Edmund with accusing eyes. 'You were going without me.'

Edmund sighed. 'Lad, where I am going is no place for you.'

'Anywhere you are going is my place, my Lord. I am your armour-bearer.'

'But, you don't understand …'

'I do. You are going to the Danish camp. Last time you took my uncle, the Lord Ulfkytel with you. Would you deny me the same right?'

'No, lad, I would not deny you. But this will not be like the last time.'

'Maybe not, but would Ulfkytel have let you go alone?'

'Ulfkytel was old enough to know what he was doing – you are not. I do not want your death on my conscience.'

'But …'

'I mean it.' Edmund smiled. 'As I already told my Witan, even Beowulf had to face his last dragon alone.'

'No, he didn't. He had Wiglaf with him – right to the end – and you shall have me. You cannot stop me. Give me permission and I shall ride to Hoxne at your side; refuse it, and I shall follow you anyway. You speak of death. I am talking of honour, my honour. What use is my life to me without it?'

Edmund was speechless. Could this really be Leof-stan – quiet, biddable little Leofstan – defying his king for the privilege of riding to death with him? And how could he possibly argue against such devotion?

'You are right,' he conceded. 'It is not for me to deny any man his honour.' He grinned despite himself. 'Very well, young Wiglaf, rest your horse a while, then we'll go and find our dragon.'

Ivar's camp was on a hillside just east of Hoxne. To the north it commanded a clear view of the Waveney and to the south it overlooked a strip of low, marshy ground, through which a small brook flowed northward to join the river. Both the bridge over this brook and the road approaching it from the village were partly hidden from the camp by a tangle of alder and hawthorn bushes. Under this cover, Edmund and Leofstan dismounted at the western end of the bridge to consider their next move. Edmund tossed the reins of his horse to his armour-bearer.

'Take the horses down to the river and give them another drink,' he said. 'I want to have a look around.'

Leofstan led both mounts down the bank and

Edmund walked cautiously across the bridge and peered up the hill towards the Danish camp. He knew the place well. It was, or had been, a prosperous estate belonging to one of his Suffolk thanes. He wondered grimly what had become of its owners, for no doubt Ivar was now using the hall as his own quarters. He had chosen well. His dragon-ships would be beached safely behind the hill on the south bank of the river and, while one or two men might approach unseen from the village, for an army there would be no cover.

A sudden commotion under the bridge broke his train of thought. He heard a scuffling sound, several shrill screams and then Leofstan's voice shouting urgently: 'My Lord, my Lord, come quickly.'

He slid down the bank and stared in astonishment across the river. Beneath the bridge, a young man lay sprawled on his back on an outspread cloak. Leofstan's sword was pressed against his throat. By his side a girl was crouched on the ground, squawking like a demented hen. She was plainly a local girl, while the boy had the look of one of Ivar's Danes – and it was obvious what they had been up to when Leofstan disturbed them.

The young armour-bearer jabbed his prisoner maliciously and flicked a glance towards his king. 'Shall I finish him off , my Lord?'

'No!' screamed the girl. 'No!' She tried to pull

Leofstan away but he fended her off with one hand. 'Stop your caterwauling,' he told her harshly, 'or I'll slit his throat.'

The young Dane glared up at him, but his face was very white. 'Do your worst,' he jeered. 'Do you think the Lord Ivar would let my death go unavenged? Kill me and ten Saxons will follow me to my grave.'

Edmund raised one eyebrow. 'I doubt if your Lord values your life quite that highly,' he said. 'But you need not fear, I do not mean to kill you. I have a better use for you. Let him up, Leofstan, but watch him closely, and you,' he turned to the weeping girl, 'go home to your mother and tell her to take better care of you in future.'

The girl hesitated, threw one last despairing glance at the boy and fled, sobbing. Leofstan reluctantly lifted his weapon. He motioned his prisoner to crawl out from under the bridge and followed him, never allowing his sword to shift more than an inch from the young man's throat. Edmund climbed up his side of the bank and crossed the river to join them.

The young Dane did not speak, but he eyed them both apprehensively, clearly wondering what fate they had in mind for him. Edmund pulled off his ring – the heavy signet ring that had been placed on his finger on the day of his coronation. He turned it over in his hand, then lifted his eyes to look at his prisoner. 'Since you say you have so much influence with the Lord Ivar, I am going to entrust you with a message for him.' He held out the ring. 'Give him this, and tell him the man who gave it to you is waiting for him at the bridge.'

He dropped the ring into the boy's hand. The young Dane stared down at it stupidly. 'I don't understand. Will he recognise it?'

'If he doesn't, his son will. I assume Sigfrid is still with him?'

'Yes.'

'Well, then, what are you waiting for?'

'You mean that is all? I am free to go?'

'And quickly, before I change my mind.'

Without another word, the boy turned and began to run. After a few steps, however, he remembered his dignity and slowed to a more arrogant stride.

Leofstan scowled after his retreating back. 'You should have let me kill him, my Lord. How do you know he will deliver your message?'

Edmund smiled. 'I know his kind. He is probably wondering even now how big a reward it will gain him, and, after all, he does not have to tell Ivar how he came by it.'

'I suppose not. So now…' Leofstan looked into the king's face and even his best efforts could not quite keep the tremor out of his voice. 'So now we sit and wait for them?'

'No,' said Edmund. 'I wait. Alone. This is as far as you may come.'

'But …'

'I know. I promised. Only…'

'You do not trust me, do you?' Leofstan was bitter in his hurt. 'You are afraid I may turn coward on you, that I may shame you before your enemies.'

'No, Leofstan, I am afraid I may shame myself. I want no witnesses.'

Leofstan buried his face in his hands and stood for a long while saying nothing. Then, at last, he lifted his head. 'Shall I take both the horses with me, my Lord?'

'Thank you, Leofstan.'

Without a word, the boy gathered the reins of both mounts and set off towards the village. He stopped once and turned as if to call goodbye, but no sound came from his mouth. Edmund watched until he was out of sight, then sat down in the shelter of the bridge to wait.

☙ ☙ ☙

In the village, Leofstan made straight for the smithy. 'A silver coin,' he told the blacksmith, 'a silver coin if you will mind these horses for me until I return for them.'

The man looked at him suspiciously. 'They aren't stolen, are they?'

'Of course not!' Leofstan was indignant.

'Hmm.' The smith didn't sound altogether convinced. He looked the boy up and down for a long time, taking in his clothes, his sword, his general appearance, but at last seemed to decide he was worth taking a risk on. 'Very well,' he said, 'let's see the colour of your money.'

Leofstan paid him hastily, and then, avoiding the road and keeping close to the cover of the trees, made his way quickly back towards the hill. He was in an agony of conscience. What he was doing was wrong. He knew it, yet inside him a small unshakable voice insisted it was how it had to be. Something terrible was going to happen here today; something of which legends were made. Someone had to be there to witness it – to know, to tell what really happened. He had been Edmund's armour-bearer, now he must be his truth-bearer. This thing had to be remembered.

Wriggling through the grass and darting from one sparse cover to another, he came at last to a clump of hawthorn bushes, from where he could spy unseen on the Danish camp. Pulling his cloak tightly around him, he leaned his back against a tree trunk, and settled in for what he guessed would be a long, cold vigil.

15

THE BLOODEAGLE

Ivar walked around his prisoner slowly, like a wolf circling its prey.

'So,' he said. 'It *is* you. I doubted it, but Sigfrid assured me he recognised the ring.' He curled his lip into a sneer. 'And what terms have you come to offer me this time?'

Edmund did not answer.

'What, no arrogance? No defiance? Could it possibly be that you have come to beg for mercy?'

Another silence.

Doesn't he understand his danger? wondered Sigfrid. Doesn't he realise he is beaten – that his kingdom is defenceless and his very life lies like a moth in the palm of my father's hand? It seemed astounding that the man could be so obtuse, or so arrogant. Yet, almost despite himself, he found he kept hoping the East Anglian would not compromise.

As if aware of his thoughts, Edmund suddenly turned to look at him. 'So,' he said softly. 'We meet again, Sigfrid Ivarsson. Last time we parted, I recall you making a certain promise. Is it the keeping of that promise that has brought you here today?'

'Yes,' said Sigfrid, and then wondered why he had needed to say it so defiantly.

Edmund looked him up and down carefully. 'Then I hope you are strong enough and courageous enough to make a good job of it.'

How could he have known? How could he possibly have guessed that those very fears had been coursing through Sigfrid's own mind ever since his father had promised him this honour? He studied his prospective victim. The East Anglian king had not changed in three years. He was as strong and as good to look at as ever – the golden aurochs of Ubbe's runes. And he had courage. If he was afraid, it did not show in his face. One could not ask for a more perfect offering. But to give a man to Odin with the rites of the bloodeagle was not like killing him in battle. It had to be done properly, with flair, with precision. Suppose he botched it? Sigfrid laid his hand on the hilt of *TruthSeeker*. *Help me, Lord Odin. Let me not fail you in this test* . 'You will see my strength,' he said coldly. 'This evening, as the sun goes down, you will see my strength, and my courage.'

Ivar was losing patience. 'You are a fool, Saxon,' he swore. 'You know what is going to happen to you. Is that what you want? Is it what East Anglia wants? When Sigfrid here has split open your back and ripped your lungs out for the ravens to devour, will your people thank you for it? Will they praise you for dying and leaving them to the mercy of their enemies? Hel's teeth, man, it's a king they need, not a bloodied corpse!'

'As Egbert is king in Northumbria? Kings are expendable, honour is not. I will not deliver East Anglia into the hands of a heathen.'

'I shall take it, anyway.'

'Perhaps, but not with my consent.'

Ivar's face flushed. Sigfrid saw his hands twitch and knew he was only restraining himself with effort. For the first time it dawned on him what was really at stake here; what had really driven his father to this confrontation. It was not just his vow to Odin – sacred though that was – it was something more basic, more personal. The East Anglian king had outwitted Ivar. He had humiliated him before all his followers. He had to be punished. For Ivar it was not enough that Edmund should die. First he had to be broken – driven to his knees and bludgeoned into unconditional surrender. He had to be defeated.

'You are a fool!' repeated Ivar. His voice had risen to a shout. 'A stubborn, arrogant, bloody-minded fool. What can you hope to gain by such bullheadedness?'

Edmund smiled. 'Nothing you would ever understand, Ivar Ragnarsson.'

It was too much. Ivar's fist exploded into the East Anglian's face and sent him sprawling. 'Keep your honour, then. Keep your useless Christian arrogance. You'll sing to a different tune this evening.'

He turned and stalked back up the hill. His men looked at one another, then at their prisoner. 'My Lord,' one of them called out, 'what do you wish us to do with him?'

Ivar spun around. 'Do with him?' he roared. 'Do whatever you thundering well like. Just make sure he's still alive at sunset!'

They dragged Edmund back to the camp and tied him to a tree. A crowd began to gather, but Sigfrid did not join them. He had no heart for what they had in mind. This was not merely some prisoner to be made sport of. This was a victim – *his* victim – the offering that would bring him truth, and mark the end of his journey from boyhood to manhood. It had been a long journey and it had begun, even as it would end, with a sword. But the act that had given him Hoskuld's sword had been a shabby affair. This one had to be different – it had to be glorious and meaningful. Would it not be demeaned if the victim were already mutilated?

He wanted to explain this to Ivar, but he suspected his father would not understand. 'It is the act that counts,' he had once said, 'not the spectacle.' Besides, Ivar wanted Edmund to suffer – to grovel and howl even as Aelle had done. If pressed he might lose his temper and decide to perform the ritual himself.

No, it was probably wisest to let matters rest. Instead Sigfrid took *TruthSeeker* to the blacksmith's and watched while the smith sharpened it. The man whistled cheerfully as he ground the blade, holding it up every now and then to squint along the edge. He worked swiftly and confidently. 'There,' he said at last, handing it back. 'Sharp as the east wind, it is now. Take a man's head off at one blow, if you were minded to.'

Sigfrid smiled. He swung the weapon experimentally and thrilled again to the perfect balance of the blade. His spirits rose. Odin was with him. All was going to be well. With the sword in his hand he made his way back to his tent and there, to his surprise, he found his father waiting for him. Ivar smiled. 'So, you have come from the smithy?'

'Yes,' he said.

'And *TruthSeeker* is ready and eager?'

'She sings like a bird in my hand.'

'Good. Now you too must be made ready. I have ordered my men to construct a bathhouse in one of the outbuildings. I will prepare you with my own hands for your ritual.'

The sun was stubborn in its setting. It clung with thin red fingers to the horizon, searing the clouds and staining the land and the waters of the marsh with dragon's blood. Its lengthening shadows made a grotesque frost giant of the oak tree in the centre of the camp and troll figures of the men gathered around it. The group parted as Sigfrid and his father approached and Sigfrid could sense the air of expectation. He hoped nobody would know how feverishly his heart was beating.

His body felt raw, cleaner than it had ever been in his life. Over the past two hours, he had been sweated, scrubbed and switched briskly with a handful of birch twigs until his skin tingled all over. His hair had been combed, his fingernails trimmed, he was wearing a brand new helmet and chain mail byrnie. He felt like Sigurd the Volsung, striding into Lyngi's hall.

He looked around his audience and then at the sagging figure bound to the tree trunk. Edmund didn't move, and for one awful moment, Sigfrid thought he might be dead. Then someone dashed a cup of water into his face and he coughed and groaned and opened his eyes. He was a mess, bruised and bloodied, his clothes cut to ribbons by the whips and javelins they had used on him. For a moment Sigfrid was reminded of the dead wren dangling from the blacksmith's pole at Beodricesworth, but then he looked more closely. They had not touched the king's face – or his spirit. The features were still strong and beautiful, the eyes as uncompromising as ever. The sacrifice had not been cheapened.

Halfdan cut the prisoner's bonds and he collapsed in a heap at the foot of the tree. A couple of men ran forward to lift him, but he shrugged them off and hauled himself to his feet. He looked at Ivar and Ivar scowled at him. 'So,' said the Viking, 'has the taste of leather and cold steel chilled your pride? Are you willing yet to surrender your country to me?'

Edmund did not answer. His eyelids flickered and Sigfrid wondered what force of will was keeping him on his feet. Ivar pressed on remorselessly. 'You think you are strong; you think I cannot break you, but you do not yet begin to know the real meaning of pain. The man was never born who did not scream for mercy in the talons of the bloodeagle.'

There was another silence. A shudder ran through the East Anglian's body. He closed his eyes, then opened them again. 'So be it,' he said at last. 'No pain lasts forever, and afterwards … my God does not abandon his followers.'

'Ah yes, your heaven, your Christian Valhalla.' Ivar leaned forward and his eyes glittered with spite. 'But, tell me this, Saxon, will your White Christ welcome into his hall a man who has been dedicated to Odin?'

His words dropped like pebbles onto ice. Edmund stiffened. Fear, uncertainty flickered for a moment in his eyes, but then he smiled. 'Your threats are meaningless,' he said. 'I was dedicated to my God long ago, in baptism. Do you think some pagan rite can alter that?'

He sounded so confident, but did he really believe it, or was it simply one last act of defiance? Sigfrid wished he could be certain. What *did* happen to victims after death? What did Odin do with them? And how could Edmund know that his White Christ would not be jealous? Sigfrid remembered the mysterious 'state of grace' Bishop Humbert had talked about – something he had said was essential to the Christian afterlife. Could it be destroyed by the bloodeagle? And if it was, might Edmund's terrible, three-headed god cast him down forever into that pit of flames the Christians called hell?'

When you give a man to Odin … when you look into his eyes … then you will know the true meaning of victory. He looked into the eyes of Edmund of East Anglia. No, this wasn't victory. This was … he groped to find a word for what his heart was telling him. This was wrong, intrinsically and unequivocally wrong. It crossed some unspoken boundary of what was permissible. Edmund was a great man, a hero, the bravest he had ever met. No one had the right to destroy a man like that. You might torture him, you might even take his life, but to condemn his spirit to the underworld ... Niflheim would only last until Ragnarok, the Christian hell went on forever.

A knife twisted in his heart. He had been cheated again. If this was his truth, the great wisdom he had been promised, then he didn't want it. It was too hard, too uncompromising. But it was here and somehow he had to deal with it.

'Prepare him for sacrifice,' ordered Ivar.

Two men carried over a door they had wrenched from one of the outbuildings. They wedged it at an angle against the tree trunk and drove pegs into the ground in front of it, to stop it slipping. Into the top corners they hammered two iron spikes. The onlookers pressed in closer. Halfdan dragged his prisoner to the makeshift altar and, throwing him against it on his knees, lashed his upstretched arms to the iron spikes. He drove another peg into the ground at Edmund's feet and bound his ankles to it. Then, using his knife, he stripped away the tattered remnants of the victim's shirt. 'It is done,' he said.

Ivar looked at Sigfrid. He smiled. 'He is all yours now.

Do it well.'

Sigfrid moved into position behind his victim. He felt trapped. His mind was a thunderstorm of confusion. He looked at his father, but Ivar's face had already taken on its Asgard look. He stared into the blood-hungry faces of his audience. Help me, he wanted to cry. Show me what I must do. But there was nobody to appeal to.

Edmund was silent. His body twitched and the muscles of his back quivered like overstretched bow strings. What must be going through his mind? And every moment of delay would only add to his agony. Like one acting in his sleep, Sigfrid laid his hand to the hilt of *TruthSeeker*.

And suddenly the world righted itself. The blade sang as it came out of the sheath, and the sound cleared his confusion like a wind blowing away fog. At last he knew what he had to do. He remembered the words the blacksmith had spoken as he handed back the newly sharpened weapon: ' ... *take a man's head off at one blow, if you were minded to.*'

Clasping *TruthSeeker* with both hands, he reached out and touched the tip of the blade to Edmund's neck – at the base, just where the shoulders joined the spine. He made a small, sideways chopping motion and hoped the East Anglian understood. Then he straightened. 'Go in peace to your God,' he said, and swung the blade with all his strength.

HISTORICAL BACKGROUND

The earliest written account of the death of Edmund of East Anglia was produced just over a century after the event by a monk named Abbo of Fleury. Abbo claimed to have heard the story from Archbishop Dunstan. Many years before, Dunstan had been present when the story was related to King Athelstan by an old man who had been Edmund's armour-bearer and a witness to the events of that fateful day at Hoxne (20 November 869). Abbo did not give the armour-bearer's name so I invented one for him, and he became the Leofstan of this book.

Viking activity in the British Isles seems to have started towards the end of the eight century. The first accounts of Viking raids on Ireland were recorded in the year AD797 and from then on sources such as *The Annals of Ulster* document increasing attacks on monasteries throughout the country. An entry for AD837 notes Viking fleets on the

Boyne and the Liffey and raids on churches and forts on the plain of Brega. Almost as an afterthought it adds: '*First taking of Ath Cliath by the gaill (foreigners)*'.

What the annalists failed to realise was that this conquest signalled a dramatic change in Viking activity. *Ath Cliath* (the ford of the hurdles) was at that time simply a crossing place on the Liffey, but it was on this newly won piece of ground, between the rivers Liffey and the Poddle and on the shores of the *Dubh Linn* (black pool), that the invaders established a *longphort* – a fortified shore base where, for the first time, they could over-winter with their ships.

This settlement, which was later to become the town of Dublin, would have started as nothing more than a collection of tents and rough shacks within an earthen rampart. By the time of my story, some twenty-five years later, it must have grown considerably, since it could then boast two kings, Ivar and Olaf.

Originally the *longphort* belonged to Norwegian Vikings, known in the Irish annals as the '*Finn Gail*', or white foreigners. In AD853, however, after a three-day sea battle on Carlingford Lough, control passed into the hands of an invading fleet of Danes, '*Dubh Gail*', or black foreigners. This Danish fleet was possibly led by the great Ragnar Lodbrok, father to the Ivar of my story. Shortly afterwards Olaf, who is described in Irish annals as '*A son of the king of Norway*' arrived on the scene – presumably with a fleet of his own – and some compromise must have been worked out to separate Dublin into two factions: Danish and Norwegian, each ruled by its own king.

Surprisingly, this alliance seems to have worked

remarkably well. Ivar and Olaf are frequently recorded as fighting and raiding in partnership. A later, third contender, Audgils, did not fare so well, however. He was distrusted by both the others and eventually killed in AD867 by Olaf, probably in Scotland.

To what degree the settlement of Dublin would have progressed by the year AD863 is open to speculation. By that stage the permanent population would probably still have been a relatively small one, swollen each spring by the arrival of new adventurers. However, such a community, and one which was obviously growing, would already have needed some kind of urban infrastructure. Ships had to be built and maintained. Men had to be housed, fed and clothed. Trades such as those described in my book – shipbuilding, blacksmithing, woodcarving – would have been essential and there would almost certainly have been other tradesmen such as potters, leatherworkers, shoemakers and probably commercial butchers and bakers. A market would also have developed where traders from Scandinavia could buy slaves and artefacts looted from the monasteries, and the Vikings themselves could obtain imported goods such as wines, cloth, fine Frankish (German) swords, and exotic luxury goods such as jewellery and glassware.

It is hard to know how many men would, by that stage, have had wives and families living in Dublin. My guess is that in AD863 most of the ships' crews were still fairly 'undomesticated' though some of them may have taken Irish wives or concubines. Marriage among the Vikings seems to have been a fairly casual affair. Olaf is said to have left a wife behind in Norway, he is known to have had two in Dublin and took a fourth when he went to Scotland.

Whether he divorced one before marrying the next is not recorded!

Writing a novel based on the lives of these people is a tricky business. Chronicles such as *The Anglo-Saxon Chronicle* or *The Annals of Ulster* give a broad picture of events that took place in Ireland and England during the years AD863-869, the period in which *TruthSeeker* is set, but they are less reliable when it comes to identifying the protagonists, where they came from and their relationship to each other. For instance, historians are still divided as to whether the Ivar mentioned in Irish sources as a king of Dublin is the same man as the Hinguar of the Anglo Saxon chronicle, who led the great army that first invaded East Anglia in the autumn of AD865. Similarly, there is no certainty that Olaf the White is the same man as Olaf Guthrothsson, the son of Guthroth of Vestfold. If he was, then he is probably the man buried in the famous *Gokstadt* ship found in the area of Vestfold in Norway and which is now on display at the *Hall of Viking Ships* just outside Oslo.

The story of Guthroth's abduction of the daughter of King Harald of Agdir is thought to be true but any link between the house of Agdir and Audgils, the would-be third king of Dublin, is purely fictional.

Sigfrid, the hero of my book, is another enigma. There was certainly a Sigfrid who became king of Dublin after the murder of Eystein Olafsson in AD875, and he and his brother, Sitric, are said to have been 'sons of Ivar'. However, virtually nothing else is known about him.

On the English side, the story of Edmund of East Anglia is well known and probably reasonably accurate. He was revered as a saint within a decade of his death and the town of Beodricesworth was renamed Bury St Edmund's in his honour. Most historians would argue that his final confrontation with Ivar took place at Hellesdon rather than Hoxne, but they would be hard put to find an East Anglian to agree with them, and as one who grew up not two miles from Hoxne I know where my loyalties lie!

Ulfkytel probably never existed, not under that name, anyway. The name is certainly mentioned in one account, but this was written centuries after the event and the name is probably a confusion with a later Ulfkytel who commanded the East Anglian levies (troops) during the reign of Ethelred the Unready. The name is Scandinavian and would have been unlikely in the East Anglia of the 860s.

The 'bloodeagle' ritual in all its gruesomeness was not something I invented. It is described in gory detail in many different sources and does appear to have been a form of 'king-sacrifice'. Apart from Aelle of Northumbria, other possible victims include Maelguala, the king of Munster, killed by the Dublin Vikings in 859, *'his back was broken on a stone'*, and Halfdfan haleg, the son of King Harald harfagri of Norway, whose death is described in the Orkneyinga Saga.

An historical novelist has to be a bit of a detective. As I said, historians present differing theories on what really happened; my task was to sift through all these theories and make an engaging story out of the possibilities. In the end, I used as the basis for events in my story the views put forward in a book called *Scandinavian Kings In The British Isles 850-880* by Alfred P Smythe. This book was first published in 1977 and some later writers have cast doubts on a few of the author's findings.

But in a story of this kind, a novel, the writer is not bound by the same rules as the historian when it comes to facts and 'the truth, the whole truth'. What she is required to do is to create a story of people and events that will keep the reader turning the pages to find out what happens next.

As for me, I shall remain forever indebted to Alfred P Smythe, whom, incidentally, I have never met, for presenting me with such fascinating possibilities.

Deborah Lisson
September 2001

GLOSSARY

Aesir The family of Gods, led by Odin, who inhabited
Asgard

Asgard The home of the Aesir Gods

Balder Son of Odin, a Norse God

Beowulf Hero of an Anglo-Saxon epic poem

Berserker A Viking warrior who could work himself into a
frenzied rage during a battle

Dubh Linn The black pool from which Dublin took its
name. Site of the first Viking encampment on the Liffey

Ealdorman Royal councillor

Fafnir The dragon killed by Sigurd in 'Volsunga Saga'

Fenrir Wolf offspring of Loki – one of the evil beings that
will attack and overcome the Gods at Ragnarok

Freyr Norse God

Fyrd Anglo-Saxon army

Hel The giantess who ruled the underworld kingdom of Niflheim

Hermod Who followed Balder down to the underworld to plead for his return

Hnaftaefl A board game similar to chess

Holm-gang A fight to the death to settle a blood-feud – literally an 'island-going' so called because such fights usually took place on an island

Loki Norse God – a trickster and troublemaker

Longphort A fortified base for Viking longships

Lyngi A Norse king, killed in his own hall by Sigurd the Volsung

Menhir A standing stone

Mimir Giver of wisdom – guardian of the spring bearing his name beneath the roots of Yggdrasil

Niflheim The Norse underworld

Norns 'The weavers of destiny' who guarded Yggdrasil

Odin Father of the Gods

Ragnarok 'Twilight of the Gods' – the day on which the worlds of both men and gods would end in chaos

Ratatosk A squirrel employed by the serpent and eagle of Yggdrasil to carry insulting messages beween them

Runes Originally an alphabet used for carving on stone or wood, the runes were also 'cast' and 'read' to foretell the future

Sigurd The Volsung (Also known as 'Dragonslayer'). Hero of 'Volsunga Saga'

Skald A poet or songmaker

Thor Norse God of Thunder. Possessor of a magic hammer

Thrall A slave

Tyr Norse God. Had his hand bitten off by the Fenrir wolf

Usquebaugh Whiskey (from *uisce beatha*, the water of life)

Valhalla Hall in Asgard to which warriors went after death

Valkyries 'Choosers of the dead'. Odin's handmaidens whose job it was to gather fallen warriors off the battlefield and escort them to Valhalla

Vanir A family of Gods, rivals to the Gods of Asgard (Freyr was one of the Vanir)

Wiglaf Companion of Beowulf, the only man not to desert him in final battle

Witan The council of thanes and ealdormen advising an Anglo-Saxon king

Yggdrasil The 'Tree of Life' in Norse mythology